The First Mrs. Rochester and Her Husband

M. C. Smith

ISBN: 1481099124
ISBN-13: 978-1481099127

DEDICATION

To Amanda Hutchinson for planting the self-publishing seed

To James Kachel for encouraging me throughout the first draft

To Mary Margaret Koch for offering helpful suggestions and reassuring me that my effort was not in vain

To Amanda Stanley for proofreading the final draft

To Johnny Crider, Theresa Fairchild, Elizabeth Fritz Jones, and Allen Elliotte among others who periodically have pestered me to write a novel for years

CONTENTS

ACKNOWLEDGMENTS

What Jane Austen Ate And Charles Dickens Knew: From Fox Hunting To Whist-the Facts Of Daily Life In Nineteenth-Century England by Daniel Pool was an invaluable resource.

The Jane Austen's World blog also helped with Regency era details.

PROLOGUE

Not home. Not home. This place is not my home. Why did he bring me here? It is cold, so often cold. No flowers. No breeze. The fruits I loved all gone. No family. No friend. No one who loves me. Just this ugly room with not even a pane of glass so that I might see the sky. This place is not my home. I have waited year after year— how many of them I cannot recall— but he will not take me home. If he hates me and does not want me to live with him openly, why will he not let me go home?

14 years earlier

We are married. I have stood up in church and promised to stay with him until one of us is dead, and such a promise must be kept. Did not the nuns teach me so when I was at school? Papa finally has rid himself of me, a thirty-one year-old daughter he little thought to keep at home this long. I have wed a man I scarcely know to please Papa and my dear brother Richard, who have drawn me into the study once more before the wedding breakfast. (Funny that—a wedding breakfast after the ceremony. Papa holds tight to the English ways, so no feast with wine will mark this occasion. How like him to spare the expense in any case.) Papa and Richard—poor Richard who now will have no one to make him laugh during dinner—declare it is a lucky match for me as they stand over me. I must be modest and dutiful they say. I must be a good wife they tell me. I must give him no reason to think me bad or tainted. How they lecture me! I must be proper and obedient, or I will disappear like Maman. *Pretty, pretty* Maman, *where did you go? You would have been pleased at how I look today, so much like the portrait of you that once hung in the drawing room. Even that image of you is gone. Why?*

I would have preferred to wed Alphonse, but such a thing could not have been borne, even I must admit. Alphonse is handsome but cannot keep me in a fine house, and I do not wish to be an outcast. Had I disobeyed Papa I would have been cut off from everyone else I love. I must go to this Englishman's bed tonight, this ugly man who has been so easily led by my father and his own. Perhaps I should have done as Alphonse asked and lain with him once so that I might know a real passion instead of a "wifely duty," as I have heard it called. I did not, and now I must share my body with my husband, a man from a place I shall never see. A man who adores me without the least idea who I am.

PART ONE

I

Here I stand hesitant to knock on a door, filled with trepidation and excitement in equal measure. How am I to begin? How am I to explain what I seek and my reasons for doing so? Suppose this man is not one who can keep a secret. Suppose he cannot understand the torture I have endured because I foolishly married a woman without the least idea who she was. Suppose . . . no, I must steady myself. It is mortifying and difficult to trust, yet I am left with no other option if my plan is to succeed.

"Hello, miss. Is Mr. Carter at home to visitors? Would you hand him my card and ask if I may step in to discuss an important matter with him?" She has gone, and now I must prepare myself to reveal my humiliation. I must lay bare the facts and hope this country surgeon will help me.

"Good evening, Mr. Carter. I thank you for receiving me without prior arrangement. A man in your profession must find an evening by the fire a rare thing indeed. Were it not urgent, I would not dream of intruding. However, my need is one which cannot be relieved by delay and I am required to press you for attention."

He looks an intelligent and sensible man, not many years junior to me, I would guess. His face suggests calm, and he has greeted me with civility. These are good qualities in a surgeon, one must think. Very likely it is that he holds more practical knowledge than old Dr. Symonds, the physician who was the terror of my youth with his foul tonics and bleedings. Dare I hope that I have found the ally I need?

"Mr. Carter, I have come to you for assistance. I dare not trust those who have known me and my family. This matter demands the utmost discretion. I have been out of England for roughly five years and have recently returned from the West Indies. I have brought with me a problem."

Ah. He is curious but cautious. He raises an eyebrow but waits for me to speak. It may just be that I can rely on such a man.

"You need not worry about my health. My complexion never was pale, and I have spent many hours in the Jamaican sun in recent years. My liver is quite sound. My concern is for another, who for reasons which will become clear, I am unable to present to you tonight. This person is unwell and likely to become more so. She is my wife. It pains me to humble myself before a stranger. Nonetheless, that is what I must do if you are to understand my request. My wife's ailment is . . . well, I shall be frank. My wife is mad; the medical men of Spanish Town all agree. As her mother before her, my wife must be shut away. You may wonder why I have come to you with this revelation. I shall elaborate.

"Four years ago we were wed to please our families more than ourselves. Does my bluntness shock you? I must speak honestly if you are to comprehend my situation. Not until the nuptials had been over some weeks did I learn that my mother-in-law lived, if you can call it that, in a state of hopeless violence and instability. At first I forgave the omission, for I could understand how no decent family would be glad to share such embarrassing information with a prospective suitor. Mr. Mason, my father-in-law, was an acquaintance of long standing of my own father, and I little imagined that he could remain silent out of malicious intent. However, as time passed, I began to have misgivings, particularly when I learned of a second Mason who was kept from view. There is a younger son woefully deficient in intellect and incapable of living with the family. Gradually, I saw qualities in my wife which disquieted me at first and then finally taught me the full measure of degradation. Honor forbids me for mentioning specifics, but suffice it to say that I am bound to one who will never be the chaste, temperate and loving partner one is promised during the marriage ceremony."

He was surprised when my voice rose and then broke, that much is clear. Still, he is not rattled. Oh, thank heavens for his offer of brandy. I have come to the difficult point of my speech and need a stimulant to rally me. There, now I am master of myself again and can continue.

"Mr. Carter, whatever your answer to the question I will pose momentarily, I shall remain grateful for your kindness just now. Thanks to your well-applied brandy and your thoughtful silence while I imbibed it, I have collected my thoughts and may resume my unfortunate narrative in a calmer state. You may wonder why I have come to you and shared the painful fact of my wife's condition. I shall tell you.

"In Jamaica there can be no peace for me. My wife's behavior became most despicable and most public before the doctors declared her insane. There is nowhere on the island Society has not witnessed or at least been told of her disgrace. Her shameless conduct grows in infamy with every gossiper's repetition. Scarcely could I leave my home without meeting one of her lovers. It is a situation that could be borne no more than could listening every night to the curses and howls from her rooms in our home. Home, what a misnomer that has proven! What I would give for tranquility and a real home, Mr. Carter!

"After suffering all I could withstand in the oppressive tropical heat and turmoil of my soul, I was pushed nearly to self-extinction. It is no exaggeration to say Byron might have been reading from my own heart when he wrote, 'I have known/ The fullness of humiliation, for I sunk before my vain despair, and knelt/To my own desolation.' I would wish a similar existence on no human. I could hate no one that much, not even those whose greed and deceit placed me in those straits.

"I digress and the hour grows later. Forgive me, Mr. Carter. At the nadir of my suffering, Providence—in the form of a cooling breeze—cast me a line of thought which saved my life. I recognized I was yet the master of my actions and could depart that unhappy place at will. I determined that I should return to England, where I might live at least without facing shame at every turn. My marriage is unknown here. That is one point in which my father and my brother had some sense of familial obligation, you see. They bore me little love, but their pride in the Rochester name and their abhorrence of scandal sealed their lips when I revealed the despicable behavior of my wife in a letter written soon after our marriage.

Fortunately, my material circumstances are such that I could hire a small private vessel, so I was spared the indignity of having fellow travelers learn my relationship to the swearing fiend locked in the aft cabin. I could trust no servant from Spanish Town to remain loyal or discreet, so I managed Bertha's care the best I could on my own. The ship's surgeon gave liberally of what soporifics he could spare and I dosed her with enough wine to keep her unsteady, but my wife blew a tempest unlike any the crew has seen before or shall see again. I cringe to think of how she lowered herself in filthy personal habits and filthier language beneath the most uncouth crewman. It does not do to dwell on such things.

"Thornfield Manor, the home of my youth, has come to me. You are perhaps aware that my elder brother Rowland succumbed to a fever two years ago and my father departed this world some months ago, leaving me in possession of both Thornfield and another more modest property, Ferndean Manor, some distance away. I have brought my wife with me to England, for my principles demand that I not abandon her to the family who already have demonstrated so little trustworthiness. I must see to her welfare even if she can be no true spouse to me. What I have come to ask, Mr. Carter, is that you will help me make arrangements for her care.

"You may wonder, sir, why I have come to you, rather than to an institution for such unfortunates. Again, my tattered honor holds sway. For a handsome fee, I purchased one week's liberty, Mr. Carter. The ship's surgeon and his assistant are keeping watch over my spouse on their vessel in order that I may survey what options are open to me. In these past few days I have inspected and rejected each of the establishments mentioned to me during some quiet inquiries I made in London. I was appalled by the conditions of such places, Mr. Carter. It is disgraceful that men charged with their care can chain and experiment upon fellow humans who cannot choose what they are. Equally repellent to me is the practice of allowing paying visitors into the asylums to witness the inmates' piteous condition. I cannot abide the thought of my wife, loveless though our union has been, being gawked at and mocked by strangers. Instead, I wish to place my wife in a confidential situation where she will be tended with as much tolerance and gentleness as is practical. Furthermore, there are periods when Bertha is calm and seemingly sane. In those days she is well aware of who she is and what her connection to me is. I cannot risk having her publish the truth to any audience. I must keep our marriage a secret if I am to build a life worth living. Because of my wife's violent temperament the possibility of injury to herself or whatever attendant I can bribe is ever present. Mr. Carter, it would be irresponsible and arrogant of me not to have an advisor in this matter. Furthermore, I have a hope, a very small hope, that someday the medical sciences will advance and a compassionate and useful treatment for my wife and those like her may be found. Will you be that advisor, Mr. Carter? Will you guide me in the best way to accommodate a madwoman with some dignity?

"You ask why I have entrusted you with such a secret. That is a fair question. The answer is this. I have bared my shame and my plan to you, Mr. Carter, for several reasons. First, you are the nearest surgeon to Thornfield. Knowing my wife's vicious and aggressive predilections as I do, I expect your skills will be required more than those of a physician who could do little but recommend tablets and tinctures and confirm a diagnosis which is obvious to anyone who spends more than a minute in her company. Second, Mr. Carter, you are a man still young enough to be interested for his craft. Such enthusiasm requires money, and I can provide you sufficient funds to indulge your medical curiosity for as long as my wife lives. Third, sir, I have chosen you because you are relatively new to Hay and Millcote and are known to live quietly. A gossiping *bon vivant* would never do. I will not risk exposure over claret or at the card table."

It is done. I have told all, and he must answer as he will. If he agrees to my proposal, I may yet find a tolerable existence. If he refuses, I must devise another scheme for Bertha's well-being. Naturally, Carter could not give a hasty answer. It speaks well of his character to ask for time to consider what is best to do. I will call upon him after breakfast tomorrow and hear his reply.

II

At last I may shrug off the shackles of misery and contempt which have bound me these four miserable years! Carter has agreed! The sum he asked as a retainer was so modest I insisted on doubling it. Gladly will I give it, too! Oh, to be free! Better yet, Carter knows of a woman, a certain Grace Poole, who may be a suitable attendant for Bertha. I must ride to Grimsby Retreat this very day and do my best to engage her services.

III

Why must it be so dark in this cabin? Am I never to see and feel the sun again? There is only the cry of gulls, the smell of saltwater, and the rocking of the boat under my feet. Twice a day those men come to force the vile concoction down my throat and leave me bland stew and stale water. They are too clever to leave me a fork or a knife, I suppose. When I first surmised that he had left me here, I tried to be friendly with my guards as I have learned how since my marriage, but they looked at me as if I were a dangerous animal and would not my accept my invitations. Next, I attempted to push past them, to shake off their callused hands from my arms and go out into the light. They were too strong and too skilled at trying knots in the rope they used to restrain me till my anger passed. There is no more wine they say. I must rest and be of good cheer they tell me. Soon my new home will be ready for me they claim. I hate them almost as much as I hate that ugly man, my husband, Edward Rochester. Why did he bring me across an ocean only to abandon me to unfamiliar men? After all his ranting in Jamaica about how improper it was for me to be alone in male company, this hardly seems fair!

IV

I must have slept. It is darker than ever in this stifling space. What woke me? There is a commotion on the deck and feet are tramping this way. Ah, yes, my husband has come for me after all. I recognize his voice. Shall I greet him as he deserves? Of course, I shall.

I fly at him when the door opens, ready to dig my fingernails into his face, but I am unsteady and tangle my fingers in his collar and his cravat instead. I flail and slap and call him every swear word I know in English and French. He does not fight back; he never will fight back. If he loathes me enough to imprison me, why will he not meet my wrath with his own? Why will he not use his strong hands to choke the life from me and let this agony end? He is a well-built man and could finish me if he wanted. Instead, he pins my arms to my sides and holds me tightly. This marital embrace is a mockery. He is detached and dispassionate. He always has been, even in our bed when there was no one to see or hear what we were about. This Englishman is not at all like Alphonse, Felix, Alec, Theo and others I have known. He has no fire for me; he is cool and distant. He pities me; I can see it in his expression. He pities me! Ha!

My captors of the last few days rush to his aid with their damned ropes. My hair has fallen into my eyes and my shift is damp with sweat and torn from my left shoulder. I am spent and only can pant and curse them all with what breath I can spare. No! No! They are at me with that small blue bottle again. A rough hand forces my jaw open and then squeezes it closed after the bottle's contents have been tipped into my mouth. My nose is pinched shut. I must swallow the bitter fluid or suffocate. Not this! Not the sleep that is not rest! Not the bad dreams and memories of Maman! *Everything gets mixed up in these dreams. They confuse and frighten me.*

I am a child and playing hide and go seek with Dick and Maman *in the garden. It is sunny and we are merry together . . . . My face smarts from Papa's slap when he strikes me for sampling the port left behind after dinner last night, something no proper young lady should do. He says I am just like my mother, as if that were a bad thing. How could it be bad to resemble* Maman, *who was so lively and beautiful? . . . . I am with Alphonse and his kisses are sticky and sweet with the mango we have shared. He licks the juice from my fingers, and my heart leaps. I wish we did not have to hide our love. I wish I could always be with him . . . . There is a frightful storm over the island. The wind rips at the shutters and thrashes the trees. Lightning dances across the sky and makes everything look strange. A downpour lashes the windows and gurgles angrily in the gutters. This is not the soothing afternoon rain that patters and lulls me during my naps. I cannot sleep. I am afraid, and I go through the house trying to find* Maman, *but she is gone. Where has she gone? I cannot be safe without her.* Maman*!* Maman, *I need you!*

V

It is settled. Bertha is installed at Thornfield, locked into a hidden room on the third story. The attics there are rarely used, and the door to her cell shall be kept covered by a tapestry some long-dead Rochester wife wove to pass the time. To convey Bertha to Thornfield, Mrs. Poole and her son secured the patient within a closed and curtained carriage belonging to the Grimsby Retreat and drove her here. To clear the way for my wife's arrival, I sent all members of the household to Hay for market day with extra coins and orders to enjoy themselves fully. Judging by her pursed lips, my faithful Mrs. Fairfax did not approve of my generosity. Nonetheless, she kept her respectable opinion to herself, as she was eager to spend the day visiting some old acquaintances in Millcote. With the hall emptied, my bride—what a cruel joke!—took up residence in her new home without interference. Were the situation not so grim, I would laugh at the horror my father would have felt had he witnessed the arrival of the daughter-in-law he selected unseen and from afar.

This Grace Poole is an unusual woman. Her years at the retreat have trained her well. Her plain countenance remained inscrutable through all poor Bertha's sobbing, screeching, and frantic attempts to bite and kick her way to liberty as she was dragged up the stairs to her cell. Mrs. Poole calmly blocked what blows she could and shrugged off the rest. I saw no sign in her that she would retaliate in kind when left alone with her hostile patient. Mrs. Poole understands that I wish my wife to be restrained only when necessary, that I want Bertha to be fed and washed and treated as kindly as she herself will allow. It will be no easy task to nursemaid a full-grown maniac, but Mrs. Poole is eager to fill her purse and will tolerate much to do it. I do not begrudge her a ha'penny. Pray she can be relied upon to do her duty discreetly for as long as it is required.

I had some difficulty in devising a plausible excuse for introducing Grace Poole to the servants and Mrs. Fairfax. It would be absurd to hope that no one at Thornfield will become aware of the attic's new inmate. I settled upon telling Mrs. Fairfax something which is in some respects accurate—that I had brought back from Jamaica a woman under my family's protection. This unfortunate creature had contracted an incurable ailment in the tropical clime and must have a change of environment and a private nurse. With her distrust of foreigners and her fear of contagion, it is improbable Mrs. Fairfax will approach Bertha and learn anything inconvenient regarding her true identity—particularly since I laid a sternly worded injunction on any meddling. Mindful of her sincerity and dignity, she keeps aloof from the servants and will tell them nothing untoward. They all may speculate about Bertha's origins and my reasons for keeping her at Thornfield, but I trust their wildest surmises will not arrive at the truth

PART TWO

I

I have been established at Mivart's in London for six weeks. Despite the luxury and convenience of my accommodations and the satisfaction I take in rediscovering the habits of my native country, already I have wearied of the city. I thought to amuse myself among friends from university days and to rejoin society, but there is no enjoyment to be had here. The trouble I must take not to reveal all that transpired in the West Indies saps my enthusiasm for conversation. I do not like to lie, so I skirt round the truth and guard my tongue carefully. My friends are too kind to say so, but they must think it peculiar that I remained four years in Spanish Town and have so little to communicate about the place.

Most of my university acquaintances have married and are growing fat in their fatherhood and prosperity. Their wives are kind to me but all too eager to throw every widow, spinster, and debutante they know into my path. The quiet dinners and stimulating conversation I had envisioned have not come to be. Thanks to the Rochester wealth and name, I am considered eligible and one evening of social obligation is succeeded by the next. It is becoming troublesome to ward off the ceaseless attacks of matchmakers, and there are moments when my patience is strained.

Alas, I see little among the women paraded before me that would induce me to marry were I the bachelor they all believe me. Some candidates are lovely indeed but have nothing to say beyond the conventional phrases drilled into their vapid minds since they first left the nursery. Others have altogether too much conversation but no liveliness and wit to balance their bluestocking pretensions. I am reminded of apposite lines from Byron's Don Juan when they pontificate on their pet topics: "Tell us, ye lords of ladies intellectual/Have they not henpecked you all?" In fairness, one must pity these would-be academics, for they have few outlets for employing their cleverness in meaningful ways.

Perhaps my disastrous marriage has left me biased toward the sex as a whole, but all the while I have stayed in town there has been only one woman who might have charmed me were my circumstances different. Her name is Miss Amanda Hutchinson. She is the only daughter of my friend Richardson's business partner. She is a comely brunette with hazel eyes and a pert manner. Miss Hutchinson is in a position many women would envy—blessed with enough money to choose the husband who suits her but not enough to draw the most desperate scoundrels to her. There is a strong independence about the young lady, tempered with good humor and propriety. She speaks sensibly of the day's events and watches the political pages with a keen eye. She can discuss what she has read with intelligence but is not averse to considering the opinions of others and deferring to greater understanding and experience. I allowed myself two dances with her after supper last night at Richardson's ball. Any more would have set tongues a-wagging, something which would have done no good for either of us. She was a delightful partner, I do not deny. Nevertheless, I cannot think of staying here and allowing an attachment to form. For one thing, it is unlikely a pleasant, well-situated young woman like Miss Hutchinson would prefer my saturnine features and often sardonic turn of mind. I have not yet learned how to be cheerful again. A handsomer man with more gaiety in his manner almost certainly would suit her better, and I would not fault her for that choice. For another, I suspect that my newborn attraction to her is born of her being unlike Bertha in every regard—lively without being raucous, decorous without being dull, well-read and capable of expressing her thoughts clearly and with conviction, interested in the world outside her drawing room and the dressmaker's shop. No, I must not take the risk of breeding expectations and gossip among our friends.

The time has come for me to go farther afield. London cannot be my home. It is too difficult to avoid the truth. The shadow of Thornfield's inmate looms too large and discovery and disgrace are too real a possibility. Besides, I have not yet sunk so low as to make myself a bigamist, and I will not trifle with the affections and hopes of any young woman just to keep myself amused.

Unlike other young men of my station, I did not embark upon a Grand Tour after taking my degree, for Father and old Mason had struck their bargain before I finished my last term. My parent would brook neither opposition nor delay; I was packed off to the West Indies within a month of coming down from Oxford. Surely no heathen chieftain ever disposed of a child for personal gain with less regret and more haste than did Arthur Rochester. I might have been a Gallic hostage sent to appease Caesar judging from the rapidity of my departure.

Ironically, since he came of age Rowland had been discouraged from wooing and marrying hastily. Father, prideful and tyrannical as ever, was adamant that Rowland make an offer of matrimony only to a lady equal in rank and fortune to the Rochesters. No mere merchant's daughter or offspring of a newly created peer was to be the next mistress of Thornfield Hall, no matter how large the purse she could bring to her husband. With such strictures and his own disagreeable and egotistical nature, it is little wonder Rowland went to his grave unwed. To my knowledge—limited by a lack of brotherly sympathy and a great expanse of ocean, I grant you—my sibling never developed an attachment to any woman who might have made him a suitable wife. Whether there was an unsuitable young miss in the background I do not know; however, I would not be surprised if such were the case. It is not difficult for me to envision Rowland making empty promises to some milkmaid or shop assistant. Ultimately, my father's resolve to maintain the family dignity and deepen our connections among our own kind has resulted only in ensuring that there will be no heirs. As my ever so charming wife and I never will produce a son, the Rochester line will end when my life does. I cannot expect her to die conveniently in time for me to marry again; quite probably she will outlive me.

Whatever the case may be, I shall have my Grand Tour soon and spare no expense in doing so, one advantage the typical pilgrim cannot boast. I shall be my own tutor and choose whatever route I like best. With no one to gratify but myself, I may linger on the Continent as long as I wish, and I intend to do so in comfort. A first-rate carriage and the best rooms will do much to set me at ease. Do I not deserve them after what I have endured? Have not I earned the right to dispense with the Rochester coin as I see fit?

Truly, I do not go abroad seeking debauchery and sensual abandonment. Drunkenness, lechery, gambling—

those are the habits of a lesser man, and I have witnessed firsthand the ruin to which a human in their grip can sink. My principles are intact despite the degraded company I have kept in recent years. I have it in mind to encounter people of wit, ability, and originality. I am desirous of tasting the piquancy of cultures new to me, of breathing in the sweet air of autonomy and new experiences. Paris, Geneva, Venice, Berlin, perhaps even far-flung St. Petersburg. . . I shall sample them all! I shall read, visit beauty spots old and new, and rejuvenate my soul. I shall live again! It is decided. Tomorrow I will make inquiries and find a passage across the Channel.

II

I was stupid and naïve when I left England. What folly made me think living highly among strangers could lead to renewal? How wrong I was! Paris has taught me nothing except bitterest disappointment and disgust at myself. I loathe the fool who greets me in the shaving glass every morning. No upstart simpleton who has come into his inheritance among bad company could have behaved more imprudently than I have. My lesson is learnt, and I will not so easily trust again. My departure from France has been so hasty I have had scarcely any time to collect my thoughts. The carriage rumbles along and I have nothing to do but consider my errors and regret them.

Upon my arrival in the great capital of fashion and culture, one of the first things I did after settling into my hotel and presenting my letter of credit at de Rothschild Frères was to purchase a subscription to the *Salle Le Peletier*. Having had limited exposure to the arts in Spanish Town, I was eager to make up for the lack and to establish myself as a man of fine tastes. What on this earth is more dangerous than good intentions? I attended the opening performance of *La Sylphilde* with buoyant anticipation and took my first steps on the path to hell.

The lavishly decorated hall was crowded from the balcony boxes to the orchestra pit, and the air was ripe with mingled perfumes. I looked about me before the ballet began, but saw nothing of especial noteworthiness in the audience. Oh, there were ample displays of the latest styles done up in extravagant silks, some of them actually becoming to the wearers. There were dashing gentlemen escorting women just this side of scandalous. There was laughter and the hum of excited conversation in several languages. Nonetheless, I felt no connection to those in attendance. I was a spectator and not a part of the spectacle. Frankly, I was somewhat relieved when the great chandeliers dimmed and the overture played.

Le Sylphilde caught my interest, seeming as it did to represent a young man manipulated into marriage. Unlike most around me who were more interested in gossiping and being seen, I watched the story develop and scanned the stage eagerly. In the *corps de ballet* was a dancer whom I noticed only because she seemed to twist her ankle at the end of the first act. I was curious to see if she would return to the stage when the curtain was raised again. She did and I felt compelled to know this young woman who must have endured no little discomfort for art's sake. Ah, it sickens me to recall such callow thoughts. Idiot that I was! It would have been better for me if she had broken her leg outright and been put down like an injured racehorse!

At the ballet's conclusion I forced myself through the press of fashionable bodies and purchased a small posy from a seller stationed on the street outside. Armed with a token of regard for the young opera-dancer who had captured my fancy, I then bribed my way backstage along with other eager gentleman. I gave no thought to how trite or ridiculous my actions must appear. I did not stop to consider how suspect my motives must seem. Even now, I believe my intentions were pure and noble, born out of loneliness and a wish to be of use.

When I first saw the object of my fascination in the general dressing room, she was draped in a voluminous wine-colored satin robe and reclining on a shabby sofa. Her left foot and ankle were bandaged and propped up by several worn cushions. Even beneath the exaggerated coloring of her stage makeup, she was a strikingly beautiful woman with fine features and blue eyes. Her hair had been freed of pins and fell about her in a glorious cloud of loose, honey-colored curls. The only imperfection was a small mole near her mouth, but somehow it added to her attractiveness. I stood there breathlessly admiring her loveliness, unaware of the commotion of dancers, wardrobe women, and others moving around me.

She did not notice my approach, for she was engaged in arguing vehemently with a man who bore an air of great self-importance. Having a better command of the French language than my average countrymen, I was able to follow the dispute. It seemed my dancer was in danger of losing her place in the company. The man, whom I gathered to be the manager, said she would not have been injured if she had been properly about her business. Had he not warned her often of her lack of focus? If she could not dance tomorrow, he would replace her. She hotly replied that she could hardly be blamed for an accident and that it was unfair of him to threaten her with dismissal when she had finished the ballet in spite of "oh so great pain"—this last whimpered pathetically. My heart swelled in outrage on her behalf. Surely no feeling man could be unsympathetic to such a brave and lovely lady. (Lady! Ha! How soon did I learn that word had been misapplied.) Ultimately, the man reiterated his demand that she attend practice on the morrow or find a position with one of the lesser Parisian companies, where she would have stayed were it not for her *other* talents. He brushed past me with a curt apology and left her to wipe away angry tears with her slender fingers.

It was the glistening tears that made me bold. I stepped forward and placed my handkerchief in her hand. She looked up, surprised, and then dabbed her eyes daintily. She softly said, "*Je vous remercie, monsieur. Vous êtes très gentil avec une femme en détresse. Je suis Celine Varens et je serai toujours reconnaissant à vous.*" She then turned a glowing smile on me and my doom was sealed. I still marvel at the confidence with which I asked her to dine with me, Parisian restaurants keeping late hours. She accepted and we passed several hours in awkward companionship. Not content with making a fool of myself for just one night, I begged the favour of her company again. She granted my wish and arranged for me to meet her several afternoons later at her apartment. (Such a visit could not be improper, she said, due to her injury and the presence of a little maid who stayed with her out of loyalty from their childhood together.) In the interim I thought of little else than my new acquaintance.

In short order, I, the sturdy and plain English oak, became the protector of the delicate and gorgeous French flower. Celine was indeed dismissed from the company, due to her sprained ankle. When I called upon her in the small room she rented from "the worst, most hardhearted landlady in all Paris," she spun me a sad tale of being without family and in danger of losing the tiny apartment. She tearfully informed me a mere member of the *corps de ballet* was not paid nearly as well as a ballerina, and jealousy had prevented her from achieving that distinction in spite of her earnest efforts and talent. Naturally, I gladly arranged for her to move with her maid to a suite in one of the better hotels. I insisted on giving her some ready money for her expenses as well. Her gratitude overflowed in compliments and promises of eternal friendship.

I am ashamed to admit that within days the moral code on which I had prided myself in London began to crack. Celine, unlike any woman I had known before, admired my looks and told me that she much preferred an athletic build to a handsome face. She was willing and made herself flagrantly available, and I was overwhelmed by the heady combination of Celine's flattery, her beauty, and my own hunger for companionship. We became lovers.

In that state we remained for many months and a child was born, a daughter she named Adele. Being the besotted moron that I was, I was not concerned that the infant bore no resemblance whatsoever to me despite my strong features and olive complexion. Adele was the image of her mother and that was enough for me to be content. Although she professed a profound love for the child, Celine quickly dispatched her to the care of a nursemaid in another part of the city. I understood such was expected, and did not trouble myself with the idea that Celine was ridding herself of an impediment to her leisure.

It is not an overstatement to say Celine had become my world. I lived chiefly to make her happy. No dress was too lavish. No bauble was too expensive. No entertainment was too frivolous. She asked and I obtained without dissent or hesitation. I could not see how far I had drifted from the honorable life I had wanted to establish when departing

England. Never did it cross my mind that our relationship was based solely on the *carte blanche* I granted her; never did I see that I had lowered myself to a buyer of flesh and its pleasures. I existed in a fantasy of my own making. Every dream must end, and mine did so abruptly.

Two nights ago I went to the suite I had rented for Celine. She had not yet returned from the evening's performance—having recently gone back to the stage for a newly formed group, no doubt hired because of the large donation I made to finance their first season. Despite the fluttering protestations of her lady's maid, I asserted my privilege to wait for her in the home I procured for my darling. Finding the quarters reeking with an abundance of floral arrangements, I determined to move a small chair onto the balcony and watch for her return. When her carriage arrived, I discovered what a colossal blockhead I had been. Celine was not alone in the carriage. She and her other lover, whom I had met in passing and without suspicion some months ago, quickly proved to me that Celine's avowed admiration for me was a lie. I found myself sickened by a jealousy that quickly transformed to rage. My passion for the deceitful little dancer died a violent and quick death in the midst of her tearful begging. I tossed at her feet all the gold in my purse, declared our relationship at an end, and arranged to meet my rival at sunrise in a private place.

I left the premises with what dignity I could muster and went to my own rooms, where I dispatched notes to my one English friend in Paris and to a surgeon, as custom dictated one should be on hand at a duel. When he arrived just after the sun peeped above the horizon, my foe was arrogant and insulting—and possibly filled with cognac to raise his courage. My hatred for him was great, but I could not bring myself to outright murder. I fired a shot into his arm and left the field unscathed after his unsteady aim sent the ball far wide of me.

Taking the time only to settle all accounts of my own and to notify Celine's creditors that I would not be satisfying their bills any longer, I have packed my belongings and begun the journey to Russia. I have no intention of setting foot in Paris again. Celine, liar and whore, may fend for herself. She may go to her wounded *vicomte* or to the devil! The child, Adele, cannot be mine, so let her be cared for by whatever usurper shared her mother's bed when I was not in it. I will not think of her again.

INTERLUDE

I

October 12, 18—

Hibiscus House, Jamaica

My dear Rochester,

I send you heartiest greetings from Jamaica. I trust that you and your sons continue to thrive. Your last letter revived numerous gay memories of our youth. Although it has been many years since we last had the pleasure of being in the same room and clasping hands, I think of you often, old friend. At times it seems that our Oxford days were mere months ago, rather than the decades of reality. I would like very much to see you again, but we have reached that time in life when a months-long voyage is not to be made lightly. Besides, I dare not leave the plantation for long. It takes a hard, practical man to make the most of sugarcane, and I despair that my son is not such. In truth, he is so easily persuaded to this way of thinking and then that one I dared not send him to our alma mater. Who knows in what mischief he would have become embroiled if I had allowed it?

I write, Arthur, to pose a question to you. It is a delicate matter, one I would not broach but for our years of friendship and mutual understanding. As you know my wife—before her removal, the painful necessity of which you are aware—presented me with three children, two of whom are still with me at

Hibiscus. Richard goes along well enough with me to lead him—although I wish him to show more firmness in character.

Bertha, on the other hand, is becoming a source of worry to me. When she first came out at seventeen, she excited much attention in Spanish Town, owing to the dark beauty she inherited from her mother. At that time I did not encourage suitors, for I did not want her to go too cheaply to an early infatuation. Now, my daughter is nearing thirty and is unwed although I have made it known I am prepared to bestow on her a fortune of £20,000. Bertha's comeliness is untarnished and I have made strenuous efforts to keep her reputation pure. However, I suspect that the truth of her mother's condition has seeped into public knowledge and no gentleman of this island will have her, knowing that she is the progeny of an insatiable and lewd creature.

What I wish to ask, Arthur, is this: have you any marital plans for your younger son, Edward? (I would not dream of requesting your elder son, Rowland, as his own security is assured and you may place him well with a highly respectable family near you.) It is the younger sons and spinster daughters who must always vex us fathers. Are you open to the possibility of sending Edward to me in hopes that he may be persuaded to marry Bertha? You have informed me in the past he will come into a small sum from the Fairfaxes but may expect only minimal support from your own funds. Bertha is some five years older than he, but I suspect the difference will not be noticed and need not be mentioned to him unless you consider it best. Would you, faithful Arthur, work with me to ensure the futures of our children by uniting them in marriage?

My dear friend, allow me to dispel any objections you may have to Bertha as the daughter of a madwoman. Thus far, Bertha has given me little trouble beyond the usual girlish whims. I have endeavored with an iron will to check any headstrong or indecent behavior, and I have no reason to think she will someday lapse into the lunacy that took Antoinetta from me. (Not a day passes that I do not regret choosing a bride in the heat of my first year on the island! My eagerness to bed Antoinetta got the better of my judgment, if you will pardon my coarseness in saying so. I rue that I did not exercise your discernment in selecting a woman like most excellent Elinor—God rest her soul.) Bertha never has been told what became of her mother, nor is she aware that her younger brother survives as a helpless imbecile, his condition perhaps caused by his mother's relentless consumption of wine and spirits throughout her increasing despite precautions exercised by all around her. I have not wanted Bertha to brood or bring on any premature distress to her mind. I naturally have shared the truth with Richard, as he must care for his mother and his siblings if I am incapacitated. I give you my most solemn pledge that, should worse come to worst and my daughter develop any of the repellent tendencies of her mother, Edward shall have complete authority over her person and how he wishes to dispose of her. She and all that came with her will be his without question or interference. I have no great affection for Bertha, I confess, so it is nothing to me to lose her company. It is just possible all will be well, and our offspring will be content with one another. I even have some expectation that your son and mine may develop a fellow feeling similar to that we have shared these twenty-odd years. Richard could benefit from a worthy friendship.

So, Arthur, that is my proposal for the union of our riches. I have every hope that you will reply favourably and shall await your answer. If you find you cannot accede to my request, I will quite understand your misgivings. I close with fondest wishes for your continued good health and prosperity.

Yours faithfully,

Jonas Mason

II

It is raining today; I hear the steady pounding on the roof. That sound makes me remember Jamaica, even if this English downpour surely is cold and dreary. I am reminded of the warm and quickly passing showers that swept over my home. I remember well. Often the brief rainfall happened when I lay down for my afternoon nap and made me feel peaceful as I drifted into comfortable sleep. It was just after one of those pleasant dozes that I first heard the name Edward Rochester.

Martine, the maid who cared for me as she had once done for Maman, *came into my room and shook me awake gently. She said Papa wished to speak to me about something very important. He did not tell her what, but he wanted me to join him in the study as soon as I made myself presentable. Martine helped me slip back into my soft muslin dress and quickly smoothed my disheveled hair with a comb. She sighed and said, "You are too pretty to be alone, my pet. You are a lovely one, the same as my precious Antoinetta." She patted my cheek and sent me downstairs.*

I hastened to the study and tapped at the door, recalling Papa's frequent instruction that civilized beings do not thrust open closed doors and burst in without welcome. Hearing his cool acknowledgement, I entered the study and quietly shut the door behind me. Papa was seated at his rosewood desk, and there was what appeared to be a lengthy letter in his hand. He silently waved me to the chair before him. Once I had settled myself and folded my hands demurely in my lap, he spoke.

"Bertha, I have news for you, and if you are sensible you will welcome it. In my hand is a letter just arrived from England. It comes from my old friend, Arthur Rochester, of whom you have heard me speak. He writes to agree to an offer I made him several months ago. In short, he has consented to send his younger son out to Jamaica. Once he arrives, Edward Rochester will woo and wed you." Papa

paused and looked at me. I carefully kept my expression neutral and replied only, "I see, Papa."

"Let there be no mistake, Bertha. You will marry this man, no matter what you think of him. I have kept you long enough, and it is time that you had a husband. Since no one tolerable in Spanish Town has seen fit to offer for you, I have made arrangements. The engagement suits his father and me, and it will go forth. I will tolerate no qualms on your part. Do you understand me, daughter?"

"Yes, Papa, I understand. I will do as you say."

"I am glad you are willing. Do not think your absurd flirtation with that upstart Alphonse St. Julien has escaped my notice. It will end immediately. I have written this afternoon to tell him he is not to set foot on my property again, nor is he to attempt contact with you at social functions. Ah, your eyes betray you, Bertha. I see the anger in them. Girl, do not think of defying me! The matter is settled."

"As you wish, Papa." I was indeed angry—at Papa and whomever had been spying on Alphonse and me although we had been discreet.

"Bertha, I am not as unfeeling as you may believe. I could have sold you to any number of widowers or degenerates within your first two seasons, but I wanted better for you than an older man with a houseful of children or one would have dragged you down with him as he frittered away your fortune. The years since have not produced a viable candidate, so I have gone to the trouble of finding an English gentleman for you. He descends from an old, affluent, and eminently respectable family. He is educated and—his father assures me—has no vicious qualities. I will not lie to you; his father states frankly Edward is not a handsome fellow. Nonetheless, he is a cut above any local man who could be bribed to take you. You will receive Edward Rochester with pleasure and accept his attentions in the most ladylike fashion you can manage. He is to find in you everything that is charming and gracious. It has been decided that his idealistic nature

would be offended if he knew the marriage is already arranged. You are not to let on that such is the case, nor are you to tell him your age. Most importantly, Bertha, you must never under any circumstances mention your unfortunate mother and the fact that she lives elsewhere."

My heart jolts at the revelation that Maman *is alive. I wish I knew where. I wish I could see her, talk to her, feel her arms around me again. I still do not understand why she left us, but it is wonderful to know that she is out in the world somewhere and not lying in a grave. Oh, what would she . . . I am recalled to the present by Papa's irritable bark.*

"Bertha! Heed my words! Your mother is gone from Hibiscus, she will never return, and that is all you need know. Do not importune me, Martine, or your brother with questions. You will get no answers. Now, let us return to the matter at hand.

"In the period before Edward Rochester's arrival, you may begin to prepare your trousseau. I will grant you an adequate sum so that you may outfit yourself with a wedding dress and other attire appropriate to your new position. Also, if you wish, you may have a half-dozen new gowns done up for his benefit, and you may wear your mother's best jewels. I plan to entertain often under the guise of welcoming the son of an old friend to our society. It is my desire that—influenced by the cheerful atmosphere of parties and your personal attractions—your suitor will prove eager and take you to the altar in a brief a time as decency allows. Is there anything you would like to ask me, daughter?"

"No, Papa. I am sure you have done your best for me, and I will be grateful. I will be glad to be a wife."

Thunder roars overhead and ends my reverie. What a fool I was then! I should have packed a bag and fled to Alphonse that night, no matter the consequences. Instead, I did my duty and will end my days unwanted and unloved in a foreign land. Oh how, I wish the rain could wash away the years and sweep me back across the sea where I belong.

III

Martine has washed and curled my dark hair, bathed and perfumed me, and carefully dressed me in a modest silk frock. Normally, such efforts are reserved for a large evening party at someone else's home. Today, however, all this exertion has been made in advance of dinner at home. My betrothed—though he does not yet know it—has arrived from England and is to dine en famille *with us Masons. Papa thought my young man might be more comfortable in a quiet home setting first. The great social dazzling shall come later, Papa says. Satisfied at last that I look my best—at least for a subdued family event—Martine turns me around in front of the long mirror in my bedroom. I can find no fault with my reflection, so I squeeze Martine's hands in gratitude and then start from the room.*

I glide down the main staircase to the first floor and stop just a few paces from the drawing room. I take a deep breath and say a silent prayer that all will go well. Papa's reaction if I am not pleasing today will be a terrible thing. I straighten my back and go into the room. Papa looks up and smiles—a rare sight. "Bertha, come in, my dear, and meet our guest. Edward Rochester, I present to you my daughter, Bertha Mason." Young Mr. Rochester rises from his seat and bows, and I follow with a graceful curtsey. As Papa has told me to in advance, I take my place in a chair across from Mr. Rochester, so that he may see me displayed in good light. Richard, who has been busy at the drinks tray, hands glasses of madeira around—Papa allows me one glass in company—and makes jolly conversation. My brother clearly is delighted to find our guest agreeable and endeavors to amuse him with stories of Jamaica and promises of glorious sights to behold. Mr. Rochester, glancing at me over the rim of his wineglass, gallantly remarks that he has seen already "some lovely sights indeed." Papa chuckles and gives me a significant look. I smile at Mr.

Rochester and then, doing my best to appear a modest girl, drop my eyes to the morocco slippers peeping from beneath my hem.

So, this is he. This is Edward Fairfax Rochester, the man I am to marry. He speaks well, I will grant Papa that much, and his manners are impeccable. His clothing is well-tailored and his cravat is faultless, but they do not mark him as a vain man. He is taller than I by an inch or two, and I am taller than most women. His shoulders are unusually broad, but he is not bulky all over. I am glad that he seems active and healthy. It would have been awful to be paired with a weakling or a man who must always be indoors. The truth is, sadly, that he is ugly. I was warned not to expect much, but I cannot help my disappointment. His hair, eyes, and complexion are dark like Alphonse's—no, no, Bertha, now is no time to be thinking of that face—but that is where the likeness ends. Mr. Rochester's features are harsh, and his hair is straight, unlike the soft waves I so admire on another. Still, when I know my future husband better, I may find him more attractive. I may learn to enjoy being held in his arms, which must be quite strong. Even if I do not, Papa has chosen my future and there is nothing I can do to change his mind. There is no hope of dissuading him; that has been made abundantly obvious since he first announced his intentions to me. There are worse things, I know, than an ugly husband. At least mine seems a gentleman in every way and will keep me in comfort and style. Also, with that grim face, it is unlikely that he will humiliate me by taking lovers among our acquaintance. If I make him love me very much, I may have my way in many things. That should not be difficult.

IV

What a damnable dream! My heart pounds as I jerk back to the present, and it takes several minutes to calm myself and realize I am in my hotel in Venice and not in the accursed West Indies. My room is stifling. I shrug out of my waistcoat and untie my cravat to get relief. I still am shaken by the vivid visit of my past, so I strip off my sweaty shirt. I go to my washstand and pour water into the basin and then splash my face, letting the blessed cool stream down my torso. Good Lord! I would not wish such a nightmare on even a most despised enemy! Steady on, man. It was not real. You are well and safe. Slowly, my breathing returns to normal. I go to the window and open it slightly before resuming my place on the bed. Lying on my back with my eyes fixed on a beam running across the ceiling, I consider what I dreamt and how it came to be.

With the airless heat in this small space, it is no wonder I was transported back to Jamaica. I hardly knew a comfortable day there in a climate so dissimilar to the one in which I was reared. Yes, that is all it was. I was overheated in my slumber and perhaps influenced by the third glass of wine I had with my luncheon. Foolish of me to let myself nap in these conditions! It is not surprising that my mind drew me to a similar situation. Still, I cannot forget that dreadful last image before I woke. Horrible vision of blood and a mangled corpse! No matter the contempt I feel for her, I could never leave her crushed and broken at my feet. I cannot think of that ghastly scene, yet I must think of *her*.

In rare moments when I am alone and cannot shake off the past, I revisit my earliest acquaintance with Bertha. I was so young then, so certain I would be a better man than my father and Rowland. I had convinced myself that living half a world away from them would liberate me from the old hurts and lasting effects of their never-ending criticism. I believed that, though Father had sent me away with orders not to return unless I could live as a gentleman without his support, I would be happy in the New World, my new world.

The first time I saw Bertha was at her father's house, Hibiscus. I was newly arrived in Jamaica and had been invited to dine with Mr. Jonas Mason and his family. I recall the carriage rolling sedately up the long drive to the house and halting beneath the *porte cochere.* I hardly noticed the humid heat at first because I was so taken with the exotic flowers that flourished around me. I had never seen such colors and shapes combined, and the scent they emitted seemed unearthly to me.

As I alit from the brougham that had been sent for me, I was greeted by the butler, Maxwell. He led me into the house with the utmost dignity, almost as proud as if this home were his own. He silently crossed the hall into the drawing room and announced my arrival solemnly before slipping away almost imperceptibly. (I smile as I recall Maxwell's diligence and propriety in the face of the histrionic episodes he witnessed in succeeding years.)

I found myself in a pleasantly decorated room which held familiar furniture constructed from unfamiliar woods. With me were two gentlemen, one decidedly past his youth and the other near my own age. I bowed to them. The elder Mr. Mason greeted me courteously and rose to shake my hand. He remarked upon his years of friendship with my father and a similarity in my countenance to that of my pater. I responded with the usual pleasantries and then turned to the junior Mason. Richard, or Dick, as he would have me call him, gripped my hand manfully and pumped my arm enthusiastically. He spoke of his hopes for our friendship and offered to show me all the best parts of Spanish Town and the island as a whole. My heart was warmed by his kind welcome. The voyage to the West Indies had been a lonely time for me, and I was glad of a hospitable companion in my new home. I thanked him most sincerely and placed myself at his disposal. Dick was engaged in relating some of his favourite local haunts when there was a rustle at the door. I glanced up and found my attention arrested by a lovely young woman. Mr. Mason introduced us and I did my best not to gape while bowing correctly.

Bertha Mason, when I saw her first, was standing just inside the drawing room. The afternoon sun fell across her in stripes of light and dark, as the shutters were half-closed the keep the house cool. The effect was heightened by the fabric of her dress which was striped in subtle shades of pale pink and puce that complemented her olive skin. She strode gracefully across the room and seated herself in a highbacked chair diagonal to mine. Without being too obvious, I took the opportunity to study her more closely.

Bertha's nearly black hair was drawn up in the back but fell about her face in soft ringlets held by a broad ribbon that matched the lighter shade of her dress. Her inky eyes were lustrous and accentuated by long lashes that seemed to sweep her cheeks when she looked down. I took in the rest of her striking face, but it was the eyes that drew me back again and again that first day. Bertha was in no way immodest as we all sipped Madeira before dinner, but there seemed to be an alluring promise in the dark depth of her eyes, and I wanted very much to know more of her. I exerted myself to be witty and attentive to all members of the party, but in truth I could think of little but how I might induce her to dance with me the next evening. Of the exotic flowers, the native birds, the sun in a very different sky, what I recall most clearly about that day is Bertha's sparkling eyes.

Like almost any inexperienced young man, I saw beauty before me, and I equated it with goodness, hope and the possibility of future love. Time cruelly has proven my youthful expectations wrong, but that first day at Hibiscus I was fascinated by my enchanting hostess. It seemed to me a boon indeed that, as a friend of the family, I would be thrown into Bertha's company often and given the advantage over any rivals. I never once suspected my "luck" was all by design and I had been ordained to court her before I knew she existed. I never once wondered why this vision of female glory was not already another man's wife. The only doubt in my mind that afternoon was whether I could persuade Miss Mason to accept my suit. I know now I saw what I was meant to see and what—lonely, young, and in a new land—I wanted to see.

PART TWO, RESUMED

III

We humans are changeable and hypocritical creatures, and I am among the worst of them. Despite my protestations and resolutions to the contrary, I am bound for Paris once more. I remain firm in my refusal to seek out and meet Celine Varens, but my conscience will not be quiet on another point. I left behind me, in my angry flight toward St. Petersburg, a child who perhaps has some claim to my care. Young Adele has only the most dubious tie to me, given her mother's inconstancy; however, it is not fair to visit a harsh judgment upon the girl, who played no part in her mother's deception and avarice.

Undoubtedly Celine keeps to her old habits and leaves her daughter in someone else's care as she sleeps through the day. A vain, self-centered opera-dancer must make an excellent employer for a nursemaid who wants no interference! When I know who the nursemaid is, it should be a matter of no difficulty to purchase admittance to the nursery. I shall visit Adele one morning and see if I can find a more definite answer to the question of her paternity. It may be that her features reveal more now that she has matured a bit. In any case, I must be assured that there is no serious neglect of the child. I cannot be easy until I am certain she is being fed, washed and clothed. I do that much for the hateful creature I left in England. Does not one who may be my offspring deserve the same?

This morning I visited Adele Varens, the issue of a dancer and an unknown father. I examined her little face carefully but still can find nothing of the Rochester or Fairfax features in it. In spite of her unsettled parentage, she is an appealing little waif, all smiles and giggles. If I believed she was indeed mine, I would . . . ah, but it is useless to consider what cannot be. In Paris with her mother she will remain.

Finding Adele's whereabouts proved easy, as I had expected. I merely called upon a society widow whose acquaintance I made during my last stay in the city. Madame Robidoux goes everywhere and knows every scrap of scandal about everyone worth knowing in Paris. In no time at all, she gushed forth all that has happened to my former lover since I departed. Of course, the news was relayed with a relish that bordered on gloating. Undoubtedly, by week's end the story of how Edward

Rochester came to her seeking his lost love will be everywhere. Bah! I do not care. I have lived through worse than being the topic of tittle-tattle.

It seems that Celine has stepped up from the disreputable *vicomte* of my day to a young marquis. New to his title and apparently as much a fool for the dancer as I was, the man has leased a house for Celine and Adele in a quiet neighborhood. Doing so must afford him the advantage of coming and going discreetly. Moreover, because he pays the servants, he is sure to be warned if Celine, no ingénue by any standard, entertains other gentlemen. Maybe the marquis is not such a fool after all. I wonder how long it will take for Celine to blunder and lose his protection. She always is grasping after something more—more admiration, more flowers, more jewels—so it is bound to happen. The pity of it is that when she goes into the gutter, Adele must go with her.

The house which Celine inhabits is happily situated adjacent to a park. Knowing that my calling there would arouse suspicion, I stationed myself on a stone bench near the park's border and waited until the nursemaid brought Adele out for a morning stroll. Francine, the young woman who cares for the child, seems decent and earnest in her desire to keep Adele clean and healthy. I probably have the marquis to thank for her selection. When I first approached her, Francine was very reticent and gripped the little one's hand tightly. It was not until I explained my nominal connection to Adele that the nursemaid lost her look of distrust. She said she was pleased to know that someone respectable—oh, the irony of being the "respectable" father of a bastard—took an interest in her charge. For a quarter-hour I questioned Francine on the circumstances of the household and Adele's care. Not surprisingly, I learned that Celine has little to do with nurturing her daughter other than selecting sumptuous little frocks and bonnets; I wish I could take that as a sign of motherly affection rather than a show of Celine's intractable vanity. All practical matters are left to Francine and the housekeeper, whom I am assured is utterly trustworthy and serves in such a scandalous establishment only because of a fierce loyalty to the marquis and his family. Overall, I am satisfied that Adele will do well if she is kept under Francine's watch.

IV

Seventy-two boards make up the first wall, the second and the third, a paneled box broken only by the Rumford fireplace set into the fourth. Six paces from one wall to another and six paces back. A plain, round brass light depending from a chain over the square table and its two ladder back chairs. Two rough beams dividing the ceiling. An oak floor with no rugs. Grace's rocking chair with its green gingham cushion. My small bed and its unadorned sheets and coarse gray woolen blanket. No windows, no decorations. That is the sum of my world now. I do not know why such a room existed in this fine house before my arrival. Perhaps some dour, self-righteous ancestor of my husband's thought to close up his rebellious young wife, hide a malformed sister, punish a scandalous daughter or keep his unwanted and tiresome mother-in-law out of sight. Perhaps there was another like me who could not help being herself and was punished for it.

My wardrobe consists of two dotted muslin dressing gowns—one for wearing and one for washing when Grace can abide its griminess no more. Ribbons, stockings, and other fripperies are part of my past. I am given neither mirror nor brush to divert myself by tidying my hair. My feet and my nails have grown rough from neglect. I have no books, no fashion plates, and no pamphlets. I am not even allowed to assist with Grace's interminable sewing and needlework although I once had some skill in embroidery and tambour work. How am I to fill the endless waking hours other than by learning every inch of this room and devising a means of leaving it forever? On days when I have been able to keep my mind still, I have passed time by surveying each detail of this room. I know the swirls and knots in each panel, the animal shapes and goblin faces that seem embedded in the wood. I know the number of links in the lamp chain. I know how many bricks line the fireplace, at least within my limited view. I even know how many stitches Grace will make before she rocks her chair forward and then back again. If I am mad as my persecutor claims, it is because I have been denied all forms of amusement and happiness! Damn him! Why did he bring me here?

I have not seen a proper bathtub since I came to this house called Thornfield—how apt! Once a week Grace heats water sufficient only to lather and rinse my naked body carefully by the fire. Less frequently, she petitions her friend Leah, whom I never have encountered because of my husband's strict decree that I must never under any circumstances be seen by anyone save himself or Carter, to help her fetch a large can of warm water to the threshold. Grace then drags the can into our room and helps me wash my hair. I am the wife of a gentleman, but I might as well live in a thatched cottage among the rabble.

I long for well-seasoned dinners and glasses of lovely, lovely Madeira. Instead, I subsist on bland soups, stews, cheeses, crusty rolls and cups of tea. Nothing that needs a knife or fork is allowed onto my tray, so I get cutlets only when my keeper feels inclined to slice my meat before bringing it to me. (Worse for the wear with gin one night, Grace told me the cook, Mary, had asked, "Why is that poor creature upstairs never to have wholesome puddings and roast on her tray?" When told that the doctors felt the patient's frail health could not take the risk, Mary had retorted angrily, "Pshaw! That shows what your physicians know! How is a body to live year after year without good English beef?" Grace guffawed at the notion of me as a delicate invalid. I wonder what she tells Leah and the others when she goes to the servants' quarters after locking me in for the night. Unless she falls asleep in her chair after a cup too many, Grace never stays with me past midnight. Generally, at that hour, she bids me good night and locks the door till morning. She says she needs to sleep without worrying what might befall her.) Most of all, these days I crave fruit, real fresh fruit. Grace now and again brings me a sliced apple or some plums from Thornfield's orchard and kitchen garden. More often, though, the only fruit I get has been stewed to a mush or added sparingly to a pastry. What I would not give for mango, papaya, paw-paw fruit, oranges—the delicious and juicy treasures of my youth!

V

When in good spirits, my Italian mistress can be most engaging company. She has a gift for imitating the voices and quirks of our acquaintances and delights in mercilessly exposing the flaws they do not find in themselves. Even I am not excepted from her ridicule. No one can be angry with her, however, when her rich laugh fills the room and she exclaims, "*E' vero! E' vero! Fare e dire cose così. Si deve ammettere che ho ragione.*" Who would dare contradict a goddess? Giacinta is blessed with almond-shaped hazel eyes, deliciously full lips, glorious auburn hair and an excruciatingly voluptuous figure. Indeed, she is a living work of art, a perfectly sculpted and tinted masterpiece. Alas, she has learned the extent of her physical assets and exploits them audaciously. She spends a fortune on silk and her seamstress—surpassing even Celine Varens in her mania for fashion—but somehow manages to appear barely dressed. She avers in complete seriousness that her God made her for His own pleasure and there is no reason He would want her to hide under clothing like an ugly spinster. Oh, she is a brazen strapper! There are moments when I can do nothing but marvel at her self-assurance.

We met in her hometown of Venice one evening when I attended alone a performance of one of Bellini's many works of that period. Perhaps it was *I Capuleti e i Montecchi*, an adaptation of Romeo and Juliet. I was standing in the lobby of the Teatro la Fenice during intermission trying to decide if I wanted to step outside to cool off when my elbow was jostled rather violently. I turned to see what was the matter, and a woman nearly fell into my arms. My first view of her was a blur of coppery hair ornately braided and an impressive bosom. I was intrigued, to say the least. She looked up with a burst of Italian I had some difficulty following—partly because that language is not my strongest and partly because of the divine face before me. After a series of halting attempts at explanation and apology, it became clear that the woman had somehow caught her slipper in the hem of her gold satin gown and stumbled. Having ascertained that she was uninjured, I offered the lady my arm and escorted her back to her place among other lovely unescorted women, leaving her with every assurance that I had been in no way inconvenienced.

Throughout the opera's second act, I was barely able to focus on the singing. Instead, my glance wandered repeatedly to the woman, who was seated below me and to my right. I was surprised to see that often her eyes were fixed on my position rather than the stage. Eager to further our acquaintance, I cudgeled my brains for an acceptable means of being properly introduced—as yet I did not know her name. Now it seems obvious to me that she was a courtesan, but at the time I perceived nothing beyond her breathtaking beauty and unabashed sensuality and merely wanted to know her better. No polite and proper solution was forthcoming to my inflamed mind, but ultimately Giacinta managed it all quite cleverly. (She boasted of her triumph the first morning we awoke together and teased me for my English notions of propriety. She refuses still to answer my request to know if she actually stumbled or if she enacted a little scene to gain the attention of a man with a prosperous look.) While I lingered at the foot of the grand staircase hoping for another glimpse, Giacinta caught sight of a decayed nobleman she knew to be received throughout Venice and scurried over to inquire if he had met the dark Englishman standing just there. Coincidentally, that elderly gentleman, Conte Aldobrandini, and I been introduced at dinner just two nights before and had enjoyed a lively conversation regarding the English Romantic poets and their view of Venice. Aside from being a brilliant raconteur, Conte Aldobrandini was the old comrade of Giacinta's great-uncle, and he had dandled her on his knee and fed her sweets when she was a girl.

Giacinta, unlike many of her compatriots, was well-born. At seventeen she had refused marriage to her father's choice and broke with her family. Left to her own devices, she turned her charm and wits to keeping herself out of the street. She once opined, "Why should I not do what I like?

I like to talk. I like to choose my own company. I like to make love. If these things please me and keep me comfortable in life, why should I be ashamed? I do not accept coins from any man who happens by; I have standards, you must know."

Her old friend was only too happy to accompany her to my post and help her ensnare a promising new conquest. Upon bowing and renewing our acquaintance, the courtly fellow smiled and told me he would be glad for me to know the incomparable Signorina Giacinta Rizzetti, whom he had been privileged to know for many years. With that formality out of the way, it was but a moment's work for Giacinta to maneuver her friend into hosting a meal the next evening by exclaiming how much she had missed his company since the passing of sainted Uncle Niccolo. Naturally, an invitation was extended to me and I readily accepted.

The dinner was attended by a small group and afforded me every opportunity to know the redhead better. When the evening ended, I offered to see Giacinta home, as the only other men of the party were well over sixty and could do little to protect her if the need arose. She accepted my chivalrous suggestion and later astonished me by kissing me full on the mouth as we stood before her door. Thus began my affair with Giacinta.

As I have said, my Venetian lover is a rare treat when she is cheerful. Unfortunately, those times are becoming fewer and fewer. I have known her for six months only, yet I have begun to weary of Giacinta. Her corporeal treasures are counterbalanced by a troubling disposition of extremes. It was unwise of me to bring her from Venice to Florence, where she has no friends of her own and must constantly be demanding my attention. Despite the good education she received as a girl, she has little interest in reading, sketching, inner reflection or self-improvement. Without an audience she withholds her clever wordplay and the pithy statements that so accurately sum up the latest gossip and scandal of the city. She must be admired and amused, or Giacinta rapidly becomes irritable.

It pains me to admit it, but I tolerate Giacinta's flaws primarily because she has an extraordinary appreciation of wild, nearly primal, romping in the bedchamber. In the night she meets my desire with her own, which is unlike any I have known in a woman before. Entwined and panting, sticky and dripping with sweat, fully exhausted, I can scarce believe her eagerness for more. It is no exaggeration to say that in our brief time together I have more than supplied the lack of physical union I endured for the years since Bertha ceased to be a real wife to me. There is nothing of the modest maiden about insatiable Giacinta, to be sure. I dare not consider when, where and from whom she learned such tricks. Some mornings I stand before the mirror washing and I am taken aback by the bites and scratches across my chest and shoulders, too overwhelmed by the frenzied exertions of my cohort to have noticed their infliction as it occurred. Her fervent participation during our heated coupling may be purchased, but she dispenses it most willingly. Still, I cannot label her a whore. She truly keeps herself only to me, as I was surprised to discover when I had her followed for more than a week. I concede that such a tactic is disgraceful in a gentleman, but I have blindly trusted before and learnt my lesson. One of Giacinta's favourite remarks is "I choose, *caro*. I choose," and I have come to believe her.

It is unfortunate that Nature did not see fit to match my *inamorata*'s character to her exterior charms. In addition to her selfish moodiness, Giacinta is greedy with the money

I give her and finds every possible method of economizing in the household, so she may buy more trinkets for herself. At times our meals are nearly inedible because she refuses the cook enough allowance for good cuts from the butcher. Giacinta constantly watches the servants as if they plan to rob her and insists that they account for every candle burned and every bar of soap used in our villa. She—in contradiction to her own precarious social position—is unspeakably rude to people she thinks are beneath her in consequence and indifferent to the approval of her betters when they can be bothered to notice her. In her mind, her unearthly good looks excuse every instance of rudeness. Furthermore, Giacinta has a fiery and unreasonable temper. Just yesterday she threw a violent tantrum because I had a throbbing headache and did not wish to dine out. Within moments she smashed on the floor every porcelain and china object on which she could lay her hands. The parlor we share was soon a shambles. Not satisfied with that destruction, she tipped over a small mahogany table inlaid with maple and then threw a cut crystal vase and its roses into the fireplace. She berated me fiercely and vulgarly in her native tongue and would have scratched my face if I had not grasped her wrists in my left hand, slapped her smartly with my right, and flung her from me. Once she caught her breath amid the ruby damask sofa cushions where she landed, Giacinta threw back her head and laughed lustily. "You behave as a man at last! Your blood can boil as hot as mine, I see! Come and kiss me, *caro*. I quite like this side of you." She stretched herself suggestively across the sofa and smiled like the most unrepentant harlot who ever walked on Earth. Without a word, I left the room before my own fury could drive me to do or say anything more regrettable and uncivilized than striking her.

I was equally disgusted by Giacinta's childish fury over a declined invitation and by her evident enjoyment of being treated roughly. I also was revolted by my own reaction to her attack. Never before have I raised my hand to a woman, not even to the mad Creole amidst one of her onslaughts. No true English gentleman would do such a thing, and I will not adopt the habit simply because I am far from home and the victim is uncomplaining, nay, receptive. I see clearly now that there is too much of Bertha in Giacinta's violence and volatility. It frightens me to contemplate to what behaviors I might be driven if I keep her with me interminably. Sanity returns and I recognize that I have enjoyed her favours long enough. It is time to end our affair and be rid of her before I dispense with virtuous conduct altogether. I cannot leave Giacinta unprotected and alone in a strange city, but I have no doubt that she can take care of herself given sufficient funds. Once I have released her from any obligation to me, I am certain she will have offers aplenty for her time and talents. The only question, I suppose, is this: shall I keep her in tow long enough to return her to Venice, or shall I break with her here in Florence? It is incredible to me that I have become the sort of rake who considers leaving a woman so dispassionately. In Paris it was the ballet; in Venice it was the opera. Who would have thought the arts could lead one man into such catastrophic affairs? There must be a better way to live, but I am damned if I can find my way to it.

VI

I have awakened early, and I do not feel well. I sit on the edge of my bed and try to figure out what ails me. My skin seems papery and afire, but my hands and feet seem frozen solid. How can I be perspiring and shivering at once? I wrap myself more tightly in my single blanket and draw my extremities up under my gown, but doing so does not help me get warm. Finally, my teeth chatter so loudly that Grace looks up mid-stitch and studies me quizzically. She sets aside her latest sewing project and steps to my side. Her hand is notably cooler than my forehead. She exclaims, "Lord bless us, child! You are burning with fever! Why did you never tell me?" I have no good answer for her; I can do nothing but tremble.

Grace quickly adds another log to the bed of glowing coals in the grate and then wraps her fringed woolen shawl around my shoulders. Taking the well-known iron key from her pocket, my minder goes to the door unlocks it. She pauses to tell me that she will return soon with something to ease my discomfort and then disappears over the threshold. For the first time I can recall, I do not hear the familiar rasp of the key being turned again; however, today I am too ill to attempt an escape. I want only to feel better.

When Grace reappears after what seems a long time to me in my fevered state, she brings with her a hefty bundle which she sets in a chair safely removed from the fire. She steps back into the attic outside our door and then returns carrying a wooden tray that bears several items. Among them are a large pewter pitcher and basin and a corked bottle filled with a dark liquid. Grace sets the tray on our bare deal table and then remembers to relock the door. Turning to me, she says, "I do not believe you would flee today, but I'll not have any meddlers from below invading your privacy under the excuse of being helpful. I made two trips up the stairs to keep their prying eyes from you. Now, my dear, let us get you cool. While I am waiting for a fresh gown and these thicker blankets to air out a bit, I want you to drink some of this." From the bottle she pours a glassful of the mysterious liquid. "Do not worry, pet. This is nothing like the laudanum you have known. This is elderberry wine. It will help bring down that fever more likely than not." I am too miserable to distrust her or struggle. Any relief will be welcome, so I accept the large goblet she proffers and sip its tasty contents carefully at first and then with more relish. My nurse by necessity then fills the basin with water from the pitcher. After dipping a cloth into the basin and then wringing out the excess, she sits by me on my narrow bed and gently bathes my face and throat. The cool dampness is heavenly to me, but I am growing dizzy. Not since I have been in this house have I been allowed wine; it must be going to my head.

Something about Grace's tenderness toward me evokes Martine, someone I do not often summon up these days. I find myself trusting Grace and being glad that she is here to care for me. Grace surprises me. She is my gaoler and in the employ of that man, my husband, yet she treats me compassionately even when I am wild with rage. Now she asks if she may braid my hair to keep it off my face and neck. I nod in silent agreement. Her fingers work carefully to untangle my disheveled locks and then swiftly bring them to order. Grace tells me, "You have such thick, lovely hair. I always have envied it. If you would always be so still and good, I could have you looking like quite the lady. The master would be taken aback to see you. What would he say if he found you one day with a perfect crown of plaits and ribbons? Oh, I hope that this sickness is a brief one and I do not have to cut it."

Grace pats my hand and then goes to the fire. She shakes out a long nightgown of simple linen that has turned ivory with age and then brings it to me. "Lift your arms, Bertha. A fresh shift will do you good. The one you are wearing is soaked through and cannot be pleasant pasted to your skin. This one belonged to the late Mrs. Rochester, and I had a devil of a time getting hold of it. Leah the maid says it was one of the only things that belonged to the master's mother—your mother-in-law she would have been—that was not sent back to the Fairfaxes or given to charity when the last lady of the house perished. It has been hanging in a wardrobe in her bedchamber untouched for near about thirty years. It is lucky for us Leah remembered seeing it the last time she went over that room. No other garment in this house is as like to fit you. It is time you had some new things of your own. If only I could trust you with pins and scissors . . . Well, I shall speak with the master when next he comes home. "

I comply with Grace's instruction and allow myself to be stripped, quickly bathed with a moistened sponge, and then redressed by expert hands. Has Grace ever called me by my Christian name before? How odd it seems. She normally says few words. This morning she rattles away with whatever thought enters her head.

"Now, come here and sit by the fire in my rocking chair while I make up a better bed for you. Mrs. Fairfax can take it up with the master if she does not like me to dip into her linen press. She with her prissy ways . . . Have I not been instructed to treat you well? I know my business and will not tolerate her interference. You have as much right to be warm as anyone in this great house. I have not kept you safe through despair and violent fits just to have you succumb to a cold." Again, I do as I am bid. Is it the fever or the wine making me so docile? I stretch my icy feet toward the hearth and let the precious

heat seep into my bare toes. Why do I not have slippers and a host of dressing gowns and wrappers? Am I not a rich woman? Is that not why he married me? How silly! I shall ask Grace later. My mind wanders from clothing to watching the candle flicker in the lamp over the table. I feel listless and tired but almost happy in knowing that I will not be left to suffer alone. Such a sensation is precious to me.

In moments, Grace puts her solid arm around my waist and steadies me for the short walk to my cot. She is shorter than I, but the support is welcome. What has made me so weak? Grace somehow has made my plain bed seem inviting. I am settled amid the fine lace-tipped linen sheets—I have not slept in such luxury in so, so long—and then tucked in with a quilted cotton coverlet and a wool blanket. A hand-knotted throw is folded and placed over my feet. I am sleepy now. Grace tells me to give in and rest. She will stay with me and see that I have what I need. I feel safe and I am less miserable; the fever's grip must be weakening. I close my eyes and drift into nothingness.

Where am I? What room is this? In what bed do I lie? Where is Martine? Where is Maman? *I am thirsty, oh how thirsty! Why am I so exhausted? I want to sit up but cannot find the strength to do so. I feel as if I am being pinned to the mattress by these heavy blankets. Why are they so thick? The weather is never cold here on the island. I cry out, "*Maman*! Martine!"*

Another voice replies, a voice I recognize from somewhere but that surely does not belong in Jamaica. "Hush, dear. You are here at Thornfield. We are alone in your little room, and there is nothing to fear. Your fever is back; that is all. Here, I shall take away this woolen blanket till you are relieved. There you are. You are free to move your arms again. You will be cooler in a moment or two. Don't fret. It is evening now. You have slept the day away with no food. Would you like some tea and a slice of toast—something light for now? Shall I prop you up with pillows? I do not think you are strong enough to sit by the fire just yet."

I nod in acquiescence. I remember now. I am in England in the only room I have known of the entire country, and this is Grace. She is my companion and possibly my friend. I allow her to plump and rearrange my pillows, so I may more readily drink a cup of heavily sugared tea. My parched throat relaxes. Grace presents me with a small plate bearing cool and thickly buttered toast. I did not realize I was hungry until my first bite. How delicious this simple meal seems to me! I quickly dispatch the two slices my attendant will allow. She suggests that I should have another glass of elderberry wine first and then judge if I am fit enough for a little cake or a tart. I do not argue. To the contrary, I accept the brimming glass and imbibe its sweet contents gradually and gratefully. When I have finished, Grace smiles at me and then washes my face and neck with a moist cloth. I feel refreshed and at ease. A few minutes later I ask what kind of treat I may have and am presented a plate bearing a liberal slice of seed cake and a cherry tart. I choose the tart and nibble it between sips of more soothing tea.

Until it is time for her to take the dinner tray back downstairs, I rest quietly while Grace rocks and sews. Usually she labors in silence; tonight, though, she entertains me with personal conversation. She tells me that her son is thinking of marrying and she wants him to have a fine set of shirts and a dozen handkerchiefs, so his little bride will not have the worry for some time at least. Surely there will be babies to occupy her before long. Grace steadily goes about her business and drifts from the present to her early married days. How different from my own experience Grace's was!

She and her husband were the only occupants of their tiny cottage. They worked together to keep themselves fed. They happily welcomed a son whom they christened Martin. They later buried a daughter and then a second son. They lived on the small farm that had belonged to the Pooles for generations and got by although they never could set aside many coins for their later years. After an infected cut on his leg festered and then took her husband, Grace sold her property and joined her grown son at the Grimsby Retreat, where he had worked several years. He never had cared much for farming, so he had become an attendant. Grace said Martin was "wondrous calm with the inmates and never treated them foul, much the same he was with farm creatures since a boy" so the director gladly had given her a place at the retreat, reasoning that she must share those desirable qualities. She said she had not minded her duties although there had been moments heartbreaking and frightening aplenty.

Grace had met Mr. Carter, who attends me on occasion, when he was training with a surgeon near the retreat. Known for her steady temperament and lack of squeamishness, she had assisted him in surgery when a crazed patient escaped from his cell one day and smashed his head through a window. It was a messy operation but she had not been put off by all the blood once Mr. Carter began giving her directions for handling his instruments. He had been impressed by her composure and unquestioning obedience and had promised to do her a good turn someday if such favour was in his power. She had thanked him but not expected much from his pledge since he was but an apprentice.

The day before the master, that is, my husband had come to call on Grace she had watched a toothless old woman pull out the last of her wispy white hair and weep over a tattered rag doll she mistook for her long-dead infant. Something about that pathetic scene had played on Grace's nerves and saddened her more than she could express. For the first time, she wished to find another situation. When Edward Rochester offered her the opportunity to leave the Grimsby Retreat and lay by good wages for as long as she chose, the lure was irresistible. Within two days she had made her preparations to retrieve me from that horrible, dank ship and helped convey me here to Thornfield Hall.

Grace's voice stops. I glance over and see that she is busy rethreading her needle. How she squints at her task. She is growing old. Nay, we are growing old, for we are much the same age. My thoughts venture away from her story and into my own memories and perceptions. I recall well the struggle this plain stranger and her sturdy young son had in getting me up the staircase and into this room within a room. I think of those days and consider how time has changed us both. At first, I hated Grace. I saw her as a spy and guard. Now I do not know what to think of her. She could be my friend if she did not keep me locked in this room week after week. She has never been cruel to me despite the violence with which I have served her on occasion. We have lived together for a decade and more, but she remains a mystery in many ways. In fact, I cannot be sure if she likes me or merely pities me when she is kind, as she has been during my current illness. I wonder if she, too, resents the hours, days and weeks that she is pent up with me in this airless chamber. Will she be relieved when I am no more and she can take her hoarded gold and live as she chooses?

From my conflicted feelings toward my paid companion, my reverie meanders to the idea of women, such as Grace and the crazed woman with her doll, who have mourned children. I have not lost a child, yet I grieve in my own way. I have been cheated of the chance to be a mother. It is too late now; even if I could leave this place and find love with a man, my body has changed. If my husband had loved me, if my dalliances with others had produced a baby, what would my life have been like? I should have had a daughter. I would have loved her well. I would have cherished her in the same way Maman *doted on me. A child, a daughter. Yes, that would have been wonderful. How heavy my eyelids have grown! I wish I had a daughter. I should have had a daughter. I want to have a daughter. A daughter! A daughter! Loving and loved, perfect and sweet, large bright eyes, little pink lips and glossy dark curls. She is an adorable girl. She is everything good. She will love me no matter what anyone else says or does. She is my daughter. My own darling daughter.*

♦

Once again, I fight my way out of a deep sleep. I am exhausted, but the burning from within has subsided. I gingerly raise myself and look about the room. Grace is not here. I throw back the sheet and blankets covering me and lever myself up from the mattress. My stomach rumbles and my mouth is dry. The pitcher is gone, so Grace must have gone downstairs to fill it and bring up a meal. Will it be breakfast, or have I slept too late again? I have been sick with a fever, but that is done now. I always have had a strong constitution. In my girlhood it was rare for Martine to keep me quiet in my room and dose me with her special remedies. Oh, I hope Grace will not linger too long gossiping in the servants' hall with her friend Leah. For once, I want to eat every morsel in my dish, even if I am served another of the never-ending stews Grace fetches from the kitchen. I want to regain my robust health.

There is a peculiar sort of excitement around me today, for the sensation of independence that enveloped me in my dreams has flowed over into my waking hours. The very air seems charged almost as it is when a storm brews. I envisioned last night that I had left this room and was standing on the roof of Thornfield Hall, looking homeward. I balanced on a parapet while the wind whipped my hair and fluttered my gown about my legs. My heart beat rapidly with the thrill. The air was fresh and crisp as it filled my lungs. I heard a loving voice call my name. Suddenly, a forceful gust lifted me and I flew more easily than any bird. I flew until I touched down amidst the tropical paradise of Hibiscus Hall's garden, my idea of heaven, a place for which I have yearned since I was forcibly bundled into Papa's closed carriage and driven to the dock.

I have a premonition that someone new and important will come into my life soon, but I cannot fathom who he or she may be. I do know, however, that I must be ready. I must be on my guard and vigilant for the opportunity to meet this unknown person I am convinced will be the agent of restoring my freedom. After a decade of stagnation, I am reminded of how it feels to hope again, and the experience is marvelous! I must somehow disguise my expectant bliss, for even Grace must not suspect that I am aware of these portents. Though she has been thoughtful and gentle to me of late, I am by no means certain that she would let me go willingly and sacrifice her coveted income if she knew I thought to return to my beloved homeland. Change is coming to Thornfield Hall, and I rejoice.

VII

After an absence of many months, I find myself on Albion's shores once more, called home by business and desirous of relaxing in a house filled with familiar objects that belong to me outright. Four days ago I landed in bustling Dover. Yesterday I was in London to consult with my banker and my solicitor. This morning I wearily rattle along in a coach and anticipate my much-needed recuperation among the fragrant roses of Thornfield's garden. Along the way I have made important decisions, feasted on good, plain English cooking, and picked up a new companion for my amusement. It has been a hasty journey but one well worth the trouble, I believe.

A fortnight ago I had the good fortune to become acquainted with a sagacious financier in Geneva. Having finally ended my tempestuous relationship with Giacinta, I had departed sultry Italy for the cooler atmosphere of Switzerland. After spending several evenings in company—our hotel being somewhat empty—my new companion Herr Werner Froehle and I exhausted the conventional topics of local beauty spots, the weather, the lasting effects of Bonaparte's rampage across Europe, where we had been and where we planned to travel next. Froehle finally turned the conversation to financial matters. We had finished with dinner and cigars and were seated companionably in the hotel's spacious lounge. At first, I feared he would touch me for funds to bolster some unreliable scheme; however, he soon assured me that he was speaking with no such nefarious purpose in mind. Froehle simply enjoyed his profession and kept himself apprised of banking concerns throughout Europe and the British Isles. My Swiss friend wished to put me on my guard concerning certain Spanish American shares being promoted by various British Joint Stock Companies; he warned me that certain parties in the City were imperiling the uninformed public. Froehle strongly urged me to learn for myself where and how my funds were being used before the bubble burst and I lost my capital if it was invested there. Disturbed by what I had learned from my new acquaintance and having little else to occupy my mind, I almost immediately made preparations to return to Britain and question my advisors closely about my assets.

Like most men of my class, I depend upon a generous regular income from the proceeds of my family's agricultural and timber property. I also keep a considerable amount of money—chiefly from the dowries of my mother and my wife—in interest-bearing bonds, so that it might grow and provide reserves in case of drought or other agrarian disasters. I would prefer not to be surprised by financial upsets; therefore, I journeyed to London to ascertain just how secure my fortune remains when I travel and cannot easily agree to or refuse new ventures. Armed with pointed questions suggested by Herr Froehle, I interrogated my banker thoroughly and was relieved to learn that my fortune was safely growing. (Some months later I had cause to think warmly of Froehle, even though I had not been in danger, when MacGregor's Poyais scheme caused distress across the nation.)

Once I was reassured of the prudent management of my finances, I called at my solicitor's office and discussed with him explicitly the terms of my inheritance and how I could dispose of Thornfield Hall, Ferndean Manor, and all my other property real and personal in my own will if I had no wife or offspring. Satisfied that I fully understood my rights, I gathered my belongings from Mivart's and booked a seat on the next available coach. All this dry business is not what is foremost in my mind, however. To the contrary, I am much distracted by the squirming, slavering companion who rests beside me.

When I came off the steamship in Dover, I was attracted by an unmistakable sound I had not heard in a very long time. I looked around and found a local working man with a large wicker basket whence the racket emanated. Something about the cacophony of squealing and snarling puppies cheered my bruised heart and drew me to the noisy creatures. I strode forward and asked if I might see his pups. Touching his cap respectfully, he was all too glad to display the litter to me. The man introduced himself as Tom Casey and explained that the pups were recently weaned from their dam, a fine bitch that had come to him from a sailor friend. They were Newfoundland dogs famous for their hardiness and bravery in the water. Tom could not keep all of them, for his wife had trouble enough with their own four children and was sure to have sharp words if he did not find homes for the puppies by week's end. I reached into the basket and petted the soft, fluffy creatures. Most were solid black, but one had a variegated coat of black and white. I could not resist lifting that pup out from its fellows and holding it to my breast. The little thing nestled closer to me, looked up into my eyes, and then licked my cheek. Tom laughed mightily and declared that I had found a lifelong friend and would do well to keep him. I could not disagree and asked Tom to name his price. He asked if I would consider a crown. I gave the jovial man a half-sovereign, shook his hand, and carried off my prize wrapped in a scrap of blanket Tom could spare. At the coaching inn I negotiated a fair sum for keeping my new little companion overnight in my rooms rather than the stable and then sent a boy out for food and supplies.

As I had encountered him first in a harbour town, I thought it appropriate to name my dog Pilot. Perhaps he would help guide me through solitary hours and keep me from making poor choices out of loneliness. The young dog's earnest expression and instant trust in me touched me. I do not believe at that time I had ever met a man or a woman who gave friendship so readily and openly. Pilot saw in me a man who would do him no harm. After dining in my suite that night, I sat for at least an hour by the fire holding Pilot and stroking his silken coat. We both were peaceful and content.

♦

Pilot and I had a tolerably easy trip north to Thornfield. He slept often, possibly lulled by the swaying of our conveyance. I was grateful for his stillness since there was little room for sport in the coach. At Hay I hired a carriage and driver to take us the last miles to Thornfield. Upon my arrival, Mrs. Fairfax greeted me warmly and tittered something about how a house was happiest when its master was in residence. Although I find her effusiveness exasperating at times, in my own way, I was glad to see her as well. Thanks to advance warning by an express messenger I had commissioned the day before, my industrious housekeeper had been able to organize a fitting meal and have fresh flowers and linens put about the house. (Though it would not do to tell her, I admire my housekeeper's steadiness. She keeps Thornfield ever in readiness for my sudden arrivals, and it is rare for me to find anything amiss there.) While my trunk was taken to my bedchamber and disgorged of its contents, I took Pilot on a walk about the grounds. The dog was thrilled to be free and raced about the garden and the orchard until his energy was expended completely. If Mrs. Fairfax was discomfited by the addition of a rambunctious canine to the Thornfield family, she managed quite well to hide her unease. My request that a suitable cushion be devised for Pilot in my own room was met with a curtsey and a quiet, "Yes, Mr. Rochester. I will have Leah bring in something appropriate for the night. Tomorrow we shall look about for a long-term solution."

I must confess that I slept marvelously last night. Often Thornfield has the opposite effect upon me; nonetheless, I feel quite refreshed and in good humor this morning. A wholesome breakfast cooked just as I enjoy it has set me up for the day. In contradiction to my usual practice, I shall ride out later and call upon several members of the neighboring gentry, whom I am guilty of neglecting in years past. The business of Thornfield and my steward can wait one day, and it would be sensible of me to nurture old connections. My father would be most unhappy to learn that I have neglected the neighbors he cultivated throughout his life.

There is some legal business to be conducted, for I need to discuss a matter of suspected poaching with Mr. Eshton, the magistrate. Others would be affronted were it known I had called upon him alone among our acquaintance. Therefore, I also will pay my respects to Sir George Lynn. If he does not keep me talking—or rather listening to him talk—for hours with no polite means of escape, I shall go on to see dowager Lady Ingram and her children to offer my condolences on the loss of the late Lord Ingram since I was last in England. Truthfully, I am curious to get a look at the new Lord Ingram and especially his elder sister, who recently came out and has caused a stir due to her reputed beauty. In fact, Mrs. Fairfax could not resist gushing over fair Blanche when she brought in my tea last night. Must women always contrive to have me married? If they were allowed to arrange international affairs as quickly and neatly as they do matrimonial matters, how different this world might be!

I am sorry to learn from Mrs. Fairfax that Colonel Dent has been called away to help train the local militia in Dorset; his quiet good sense would be like balm after the self-importance of the others. His wife is a charming woman, but I anticipate that after the pomposity of Eshtons and the Ingrams I will not feel equal to passing a half-hour in her parlor without another companion. My talent for polite, conventional conversation can stretch only so far. Perhaps a note to Mrs. Dent offering her some of Mrs. Fairfax's prized raspberry jam would be tribute enough to that family until a later date.

Tomorrow I will see Mr. Pennington, my steward, to review the ledger books and discuss ideas I have concerning a plot of timber belonging to me. Afterwards, I plan to treat myself to a long and convivial conference with Carter, whose last letter was replete with news of modern techniques and equipment of which he was educated during a recent learning holiday in Edinburgh. Carter also is an appreciator of canine species, and he doubtless will be delighted with Pilot.

Keeping myself engaged with others helps me forget the reasons I have for avoiding Thornfield. As much as I might wish to avoid it, I cannot long avoid a visit to the third floor. While I was abroad, I was surprised to receive a letter from Mrs. Poole informing me that my wife had been ill for several days. It would be wrong of me to neglect Bertha. I do not love her, but I must be assured that her meals and her accommodations will not contribute to a physical decline. She cannot help what she is, and I remain her husband, however unwillingly.

VIII

I creep closer to the fire. It flickers in the iron grate and invites me nearer, bright and warm on my face. I close my eyes and pretend it is the sun, which I have not seen in a very long time. I pretend I am surrounded by flowers and lush greenery. I do my best to recall the many birdsongs that were once so familiar to me. I pretend someone I love is here, someone who loves me. Does such a person exist? Does anyone search for me or yearn for my return?

My sole companion sleeps in her chair, homely Grace who wants me to believe she is my friend. Her sewing—a plain shirt, probably for Martin, the son she mentions at times—has fallen from her hand to her knees, and her mouth hangs open as she breathes noisily. The empty mug sits on the table at her elbow. How long has she watched me hour after hour? How many days have we spent in this room, her plying her needle while I weep or rage or just lie still in my cot trying to understand what I did to deserve being trapped in this place? Many days that must total many years, I know, for my hair has grown heavy and long, and grey strands have begun to appear in hers.

I, who was once acclaimed the most handsome woman on the island and desired by many men, no longer know what I look like; I have not seen my own face almost since I was brought here. At first Grace let me have a small hand mirror and comb, so I could keep my locks neat. One day, though, while thinking about the loved ones and places I would see no more, I smashed the little looking glass and used the shards to draw blood up and down my arms. I was angry and sad all at once and trying to understand why none of those people—Dick, Alphonse, even Papa—would come for me and insist that my husband treat me well. Once I had dropped the sharp bits and subsided to the floor in tears, Grace bandaged me and told me it was wrong to do what I had done. She called it a sin. Sin. Sin. That word rings in my ears in various voices from the past. The nuns at school. My father. My husband. Grace said I must not do such things, or she would have to ask her master for leave to restrain me for my safety. She stroked my hair and talked quietly as I cried bitterly over hurts much deeper than a few scrapes that meant nothing. Later, that man Carter came and checked my wounds. He told Grace the cuts were not deep and I would be fine but should have no more glass or anything sharp since my mind had decayed to this state. What did he mean decayed? I am yet alive. How could he describe me thus? Why should I not act on my feelings? I do not understand why I must be held here and am not allowed to walk out of doors and live on my own. What have I done that is so wrong? Why must everyone be against me? Is my fate the same as Maman's? *Is she yet in a cramped, dark and chilly room waiting for her release?*

IX

Clara is a gentle soul; she gives me no trouble at all—unlike Celine and Giacinta before her. Clara, the widow of a cavalry officer, is closer to my own age than my past mistresses. She is fair and her blue eyes somehow still suggest a bewildered innocence. Her shape is that of a woman who is comfortable with her age and has a fondness for *Apfelstrudel* and *Krapfen.* I encountered her at a large musical assembly in Munich and was drawn to her composed demeanor amid the tawdry self-promotion of the other ladies of questionable virtue. Wearing a gown that obviously had done duty in seasons past, she seemed a bit sad and tired behind her fluttering fan as she stood apart from the crowd during an intermission. I felt the same and sympathized with her. With Clara, there was none of the banal romance or gamesmanship that preceded my prior arrangements. I simply went to her and asked if she would like to sit outside away from the noise and press of the crowd. She acquiesced and we talked quietly in the ornamental garden while others crowded around the punch bowl and brayed with forced hilarity. She was patient with my unsure German, and I was delighted to discover that she had learned some English in her youth because her father had been a Shakespeare enthusiast and amateur translator. Gradually Clara revealed her history to me and, lowering her eyes and sighing softly, explained she recently had been replaced by a younger woman and had come to the concert in hopes of meeting a wealthy gentleman who did not wish to be alone. I was disinclined to solitude and thought this placid woman might be the antidote to the unhappiness that hounded me. In a matter of days, we came to a convenient understanding.

Clara comes of a good country family, but her reckless husband loved cards and dice more than his bride and left her perilously poor when he fell dead over their dinner table one evening. Swayed by gratitude for a loan that finally satisfied agents who dunned her relentlessly the first half-year of her widowhood, Clara was persuaded into an unfortunate affair with one of her husband's brother officers. Her dependence grew into an unrequited love; she was crushed when she found herself pregnant and her lover refused to make her an honest woman. She found her old circle of friends closed to her once her condition could no longer be concealed. The elder wives thought her corrupted and capable of making advances to their husbands, while the younger ones feared that being tainted by association would damage the prospects of their partners. A late miscarriage was an even crueler blow. Having no surviving relatives by this time, Clara gradually relinquished all thoughts of decorum and allowed herself to drift aimlessly into a different sort of society than she had known previously. Her first sponsor, to put it delicately, was a middle-aged childless widower who treated her with benevolence and courtesy and called her his "little almost-wife," in tribute to the sensible and contented way she managed his household. They lived peacefully together for nearly a decade until his heart failed after a long walk one day. He left her a small legacy upon his death, but his house reverted to his deceased wife's family and those disapproving souls were quick to evict her. Forced to relocate to rented quarters and furnish them with secondhand purchases, Clara was discouraged to find her funds would not extend to setting up a millinery shop, which had become her secret plan for the time when she was alone again. She knew no respectable man would take her for his wife and she must find some means of support. To preserve her meager savings, she next became the mistress of a flourishing brewer who established her in rooms near his office, so he could call on her during the day and not arouse his wife's suspicions. He kept her home well-supplied with food and comforts but refused to give Clara any pocket money or jewels that she could keep when their connection ended—something he made clear would happen when he no longer found her exciting. Ultimately, Clara's benefactor encountered a younger, saucier trollop to divert him and cast off Clara a week before we met.

I pity Clara for the trouble she has endured and respect her matter-of-fact manner of living with those difficulties, but, what a trial it is that she is so very, very dull! My plump blond German reads whatever I do in English and her own tongue, but she does so ploddingly and with only a very literal comprehension. It is exceedingly tiresome to explain to her what I think the author means beyond the mere words on the page. Prose is a challenge, and I gave up poetry within a week. Even a discussion of what sites we have seen together and the people we have met during the day seems to tax her mental faculties. To her something is nice and good or old and dirty; a sublime landscape or the grandeur of antiquity escapes her. She has no gift of description, nor can she often understand the humorous remarks I attempt for her amusement. She plays well, I grant you, but with little energy or merriment. The pianoforte is simply an acceptable ladylike pastime she was taught as a girl. Most often, if I have not selected our program of entertainment for the evening, Clara prefers to sit in an easy chair wearing slippers and a comfortable flannel wrapper while embroidering birds and flowers on cushions and wall hangings for hours at a time.

Uncomplicated Clara enjoys domestic life and prefers her mug of cocoa at the fireside to any sparkling amusement I offer her. I never thought I would long for a woman to spend more of my money on her attire, but there are times when I do now. Although she is still handsome, she sometimes exhibits a disappointing preference for the dowdy. Clara thanks me graciously for my offers to set up accounts with fine dressmakers but insists that she is past her prime and there is nothing wrong with wearing clothing that is comfortable and familiar.

A part of me argues that I should feel grateful to spend my days with this calm, almost maternal woman. I do not. I find myself treating her less as a lover and more as a polite cousin who has come for a visit. I keep to my own bedchamber more often than not. Even when I do join Clara in her nest of blankets and down pillows, neither of us takes more than superficial enjoyment in the activity.

To be honest, I do not think her breathing changes all the while. She endures our lovemaking as my right to a body I have purchased, and afterwards, while she slumbers amid the disarranged bedding, I am ashamed that I have bothered her and succumbed to my carnal needs, no better than a lowly farmyard animal that ruts in the mud. Indeed, I am cognizant that in procuring the companionship of Clara and her predecessors I am no better than a common labourer buying a whore for the night. In an odd way lying with this essentially decent woman makes me feel corrupt and filled with self-contempt.

I cannot love Clara, nor do I desire her for her own merits. It must have been boredom and loneliness that made me choose her. If not ennui, I must have sought her as the perceived opposite of the women who came before her. I hardly can fathom what drove me to think I could be happy with a woman whose world revolves around her own household. Such is supposed to be the ideal, but I cannot be satisfied. She bores me, and no amount of nourishing meals and tidy environs can change that.

Clara's quietude does not soothe me. Instead, I grow more impatient by the day. If only she were brighter! If only she showed some interest in expanding her mind! If only there were a way to break my ties to the madwoman I was lured into marrying! If only this and if only that! I am sick of my own discontent. If only I could live celibate and solitary . . . that would be the best thing for me and my intrusive, lingering scruples.

Am I never to find an equal or at least a woman with brains enough to captivate me for more than six months at a time? Bah! I ask the impossible—at least among the class of female who puts her security before her self-respect. Then again, do not they all, even the chaste and respectable ones, seek protection from the man who can bid highest? If I am cynical, then I deserve to be. Only a simpleton could believe that somewhere a woman lives who embodies the attributes of propriety, intelligence, originality, and whatever other quality it is that continues to elude me—much less that she would choose for a mate a man who has lived as I have done. It cannot be; she does not exist outside of my imagination. Russia, Germany, France, and Italy . . . I have searched them all and come away with no one worthy. I am doomed to live out my days alone or with only such unsatisfactory companionship as my gold can secure. I do not know who is more degraded by such arrangements, the buyer or the seller. Certainly, neither party is bettered by the humiliating bargain.

Soon I must be rid of Clara or I shall begin to hate her outright. She deserves no such enmity from me, so it is best that I grant her a sum that will make her millinery dreams possible and detach myself from her and the Continent. Indeed, I feel drawn toward England most strongly of late. Clara's uncomplaining and phlegmatic nature—I expect none of the florid parting scenes I have endured in the past—will make discarding her relatively easy. I disgust myself. Who have I become to make such a statement without shame? Have I abandoned my integrity altogether and let the years of restless living debase me to this degree? How far I am from the refined and upright gentleman I intended to become when I departed the tropics! I have become as immoral as the creature I sought to escape. I am appalled to know the truth about myself.

X

Celine Varens is dead. I had a letter today from Madame Robidoux, the widowed Parisienne, proclaiming the information in most sympathetic terms. She is a romantic and will not believe that passionate love can and does die as easily as it germinates. She always will be convinced that my indifference to Celine has been the merest façade hiding a wounded heart. Silly woman! While I cannot celebrate Celine's demise, I also find myself remarkably untouched, considering that at one time she was the sun, the moon, and the stars to me. That was long ago—before she proved herself unworthy of my regard and I saw her for the deceitful creature she was.

My correspondent writes that Celine's last days were not joyful ones. She lost the trust and affection of the marquis by accepting the fabulous gifts and zealous attentions of a *nouveau riche* manufacturer. Having warned his paramour what would happen if he caught her being unfaithful, the marquis made certain no one of quality would receive her again once he had proof of her indiscretions. Celine was left to fend for herself and her daughter. No longer youthful and spry, she was unable to find a place dancing. She had saved nothing in ready cash, and the jewels she had collected as tribute through the years were pawned one by one until none remained. She fell by degrees from the lofty society to which she had become accustomed, and ended in the same squalid environs she inhabited when I first knew her.

No one is sure of how she kept herself and Adele once the last few francs were gone. Rumors disagree: some would have it that she entertained men in her rooms at all hours; others claim to have seen her serving drinks in a tavern. Still others avow that Celine traded on the novelty of Adele's youth and had her daughter sing and quote dramatic pieces for coins. Unquestionably, Celine deserved her degradation; nonetheless, I am saddened to consider what shameful behavior Adele must have witnessed as she followed her mother back down the social gradient. Of course, what she saw in the brighter days cannot have been very wholesome to a young, unformed character either.

Perhaps I should have done more for the girl and not left her with such an unfit guardian. Given enough money, I am sure Celine would have yielded the child to me and thought little more of her. I could have installed Adele at a good school where she would have been given some education and skills to help her later in life. I did not act then, but I may be able to do the girl some good now. Madame Robidoux reports that Adele has been taken in by a former dancer and friend of her mother and is encouraged to develop all her inherited charms however inappropriate to her age the performances may be. Though I may bear no responsibility for the child's being on this Earth, the slightest possibility that she is my flesh means that I cannot leave her to grow up in a world of ignorance, vanity and corrupt morals. There was a time when I lived happily in that sphere, but I hope I have not forgotten all the principles I held dear when I was younger.

I shall leave for Paris within the week. I shall find Adele and judge for myself whether her current home is a good one. If not, I will meet the child and learn if she is willing to live as my ward in England. I will not force her to come away with me if doing so is abhorrent to the girl. God knows Thornfield Hall needs no other unhappy souls pent within its walls.

♦

What heavy seas there were on this trip! I cannot recall a time when the Channel was so rough. I am a seasoned traveler, yet I succumbed to *mal de mer*, the same as Adele and her new nursemaid. Sophie was recommended to me by Madame Robidoux after Adele's former nurse declined to leave her own country despite the generous pay I offered. At least Adele was mostly silenced by her indisposition. In the past two weeks I have heard enough babbling about dresses, slippers, packing and the rest to make me quite loathe the French language. The only sensible company I have had has been faithful Pilot, my Newfoundland dog. What he thought of the pitching ship I cannot imagine. The poor creature just lay on the floor near my sofa and whimpered occasionally. Stepping off the gangplank onto English soil was a glorious thing for both of us, and I am certain my long-haired friend is as pleased as I to rest tonight in a room that stays still. We all will need a day of quiet here in Dover before we begin the journey to Thornfield.

What a turn of events! I, Edward Rochester, have become the protector of a little French bastard! Mrs. Fairfax will be greatly puzzled by my latest foreign acquisition, yet I trust that she will ask not one inconvenient or leading question about the girl's origins. Mrs. Fairfax is not the most intelligent housekeeper in Britain, but she excels at being all that is thoughtful, kind and respectable. I will entrust her with the arrangements for Adele's care. Yes, that will do well. I will inform Mrs. Fairfax of my intentions tomorrow evening after dinner. For a liberal sum like thirty pounds per year she should be able to find a governess with some experience and ability.

♦

Having returned to Thornfield, I find the gloomy place as insupportable as ever and cannot stay. Earlier this evening I made my dutiful visit to the third floor. The little room and its occupants are unchanged. Bertha continues to thrive in body, if not in mind. She has grown corpulent in the last few years, and her attractiveness has vanished forever. If I had ever loved her, that loss would sadden me.

I strive not to be cruel in thought or action toward her, but I am frustrated to find she likely will outlive me some day. We are bound to one another until death, so I may never live as an honest man with a decent woman and raise our family.

Bertha spat and swore when I entered the chamber but made no move to strike me, as she frequently has done before. Mrs. Poole reports that her patient has been quieter than usual of late. Maybe her declining faculties have mellowed some of the hatred she has for me as her memories fade. She never did spare me any abuse and blame for our marriage. When I recall her railing in Jamaica, the blood rushes to my cheeks, even after a decade. She was a party to the deception, so I do not know why I am a monster for allowing myself to be tricked. I do not comprehend why she is eager to hurt me when I have done my best to keep her safe.

To the deuce with these thoughts! Any exposure to that fiend upstairs darkens my view and puts me out of charity with mankind. I will not stay at Thornfield a minute more than is required to ensure the estate is being managed properly. While I am in the country it would be wise to visit Ferndean Manor as well. How long has it been since I made the trip to Ferndean? Too long, I think, since an answer does not come readily to mind. It is risky to leave one's property unattended for too long, even if it is a small and somewhat uncomfortable one. With no tenant or close neighbor to apprise me of its condition, I must not neglect the manor any longer. Perhaps I will spend a day or two in blessed solitude there before I decide upon my next destination. After all the feminine fluttering of good Mrs. Fairfax and her newly arrived cohabitants, I would welcome a quiet house most heartily. John could accompany me to Ferndean and see to what little sustenance and service I would require for a brief visit. It is unfortunate that Ferndean Manor was erected in a damp and inconvenient location. Otherwise, I might have kept my cherished spouse there and been able to occupy Thornfield Hall with less trepidation and brooding. Alternatively, I might have spent more time at Ferndean hunting with friends in due season.

Ha! I say that as if I have real friends. Besides Carter, I can lay claim to no one who deserves the title, and he is rarely able to spend more than a single day in the pursuits that seem to bond men in lifelong communion. I have been from one end of the Continent to the other, yet there is no acquaintance whose absence I genuinely regret when I have moved from city to city. It is not only the love of an upright woman that has been denied to me. I also have been barred from forming closer ties to men worthy of respect and consideration. Forever holding back an unpleasant truth about myself makes it difficult for me to fully engage in the friendship of those I meet. I do not even keep a valet for fear of trusting a man who someday will expose me. Despite wishing to feel more open, I often find myself seeing the worst aspects of those around me and suspecting they will disappoint and betray me ultimately. Even an individual as easily guided and good-natured as my brother-in-law worked against me. It seems I am to bear my troubles alone.

XI

My husband—Edward Rochester, I must remember that name so that the law might punish him for holding me here against my will—is away again. I know, for there is no traffic to the front door and he has not come to look upon me with distrust and disgust. He fears me, and he should. I would tear out his throat with my teeth if it meant I could leave this cold land and go back to my home. Yes, he is away, but the house is not as quiet as it should be in his absence. During the day I hear new voices. I hear words that take me back to my youth. Who is this child prattling brightly in the language of my precious Maman*? I cannot see the girl, but her high voice pierces even the locked heavy oak door to my room. Why is she here? He must have a plan for her, but I cannot comprehend it. Certainly she has not come alone, for there are others speaking French to one another as they move about the gallery below. The feel of this place has changed somehow. Something is going to happen. Even Grace spends more time belowstairs than watching me and doing her eternal needlework by the fire. Who are these people, and why are they moving about freely while I must stay always in my tiny cell?*

I do not have a child. At least, I do not think I have a child. Sometimes I hear a young girl in this house, but she cannot be mine, can she? Can she? There are so many things I cannot recall clearly since I came to this accursed place. The days run together, and I do not know how long I have been kept here. Still, I heard the child again this morning. I heard her laughing and singing. She spoke Maman's *language, but somehow differently. Have I dreamed her up in my loneliness? Am I as mad as he has claimed? Why should there be a little girl in this house? Is she my daughter? Did I have a baby? Did my husband take her from me? Have they—my husband, Grace, Carter—made me forget her? If she is not mine, why would he keep her near him? Are they keeping her from me the same way I was kept from* Maman*? I must know what is happening in the house below me! Grace must tell me the truth!*

I asked Grace who the child was and if she had noticed the sweet, young voice singing. Grace barely looked up from her stitching as she told me to hush. She said I must not trouble myself with things and people I cannot see. She said the girl was not present in this room, so I should forget what I thought I heard. I am confused. Does the child exist in flesh? Is she seeking me? If only Grace would leave me unattended for a while, I could call out and tell the girl where I am. I would beg her to help me. Perhaps she could find a second key and open the door. Does she know I am here, and is she using French to communicate, so the others will not understand? Oh, she must be wary. He knows the language; I recall that now. He is cruel to separate me from my daughter! Why must men be unkind to mothers and daughters and divide us? What danger do we present? Is it not enough that we must follow the rules they set all our lives? We must be pretty but not invite admiring glances too often. We must be lively but keep quiet when they are speaking. We must ask them for money and have almost none of our own. Why must we be sold into marriage? Why?

The girl, the innocent one, must be warned. If she stays here, if she does not get away before she is grown she will be trapped the way I was and my mother before me. She will be given to a stranger and then taken from those who love her best. He will not let her be happy. He will shut her away if she displeases him—and having French ways is sure to do just that. Poor, dear daughter. My poor angel I cannot hold. If only I could speak to her . . . If only I could shout loudly enough . . . I would warn her and let her learn from my misery.

PART THREE

I

Thornfield. Often have I wondered why my ancestors chose such an inhospitable name, yet such an appropriate one—at least for me. Thornfield never was meant to be my home and haven. Father made that plain enough for as long as I can recall. How often a meal was made less palatable by some variation of his pet speech to me: "I will not divide this land or the income it provides. All go to your brother. It is his right as the eldest; it is the Rochester way. You have the advantages of birth and education. You must marry well, for I will not have you disgracing me with indigence or a demeaning profession. Forget any foolish notions of love. You will wed a dowry--if you are fortunate, one bound to a woman more handsome than you." These harangues were even more disheartening in that they invariably occurred in the presence of Rowland, who smirked over the claret in smug security. No genuine filial affection could thrive in such an environment, and I was glad that primogeniture would have a hand in separating us some day, however much I envied the ease in which he could expect to live. My father's decree came to pass. He did not divide the estate, and I did marry a woman of some fortune and beauty. What would Arthur Rochester feel if he knew to what doom his rigidity has condemned me? Had I resisted my father's urgings, what might have been? What hopes would have flourished in contentment and happiness? What might I have been other than the cynical and dissipated man I have become?

I am now one-and-forty. Both my father and my brother lie mouldering in their graves. Thornfield and the family wealth are mine, yet I do not rejoice, for they came too late. Comfort will elude me all my days. I possess a house which cannot be a home and a wife whom I cannot love.

Now I may not even have the pleasure of riding out tomorrow and surveying what has changed since I was here last. My deuced ankle aches. Carter assured me there is no real harm done, but being housebound is damned inconvenient. If only he had been able to stay and talk with me, I might bear this situation with more equanimity. He must be about his business, however, so our conversation must wait. I will not trouble Mrs. Fairfax for companionship tonight. She inevitably would hover and fuss and say nothing of interest. That would be intolerable to me. Celine and her Sophie would be even less desirable, and I am not inclined to trouble myself with French. That leaves the governess, the small, plain thing who assisted me after Mesrour lost his footing and pitched me from his back. No, I will not call for the little governess tonight although something about her piques my interest. I shall instead ring for John and go to bed as Carter recommended.

II

He is here, here in his cold English house. I know, for I heard the ring and clatter of shoed hooves on stone today, something that happens only when he has come back from wherever he goes. No one else here seems to go out on horseback. When will he make his visit to my quarters and speak of me but not to me? When will he stand by my tiny fire and scowl at me in the dim light as if I were the ugly one, he who never was nor could be handsome? Why does he come at all if he does not mean to talk to me and judge for himself if I am feeling well? Grace is his paid jailer; she will tell him what she likes. It is in her interests to make him believe my condition—my condition!, a term that I do not understand—is worsening, so she may stay and draw her pay. Like others before her, she will side with him. She is not pretty. She is jealous of me. If she wants his attentions, she may have them, for I have never cared for the hideous man. I hate him. He thinks that he can control me, but he is wrong. This time I will not wait for him to make his unwelcome appearance. I will search the rooms below until I find him, and I will make him let me go. Yes, I will visit his bedchamber tonight without invitation, as he once visited mine. Will not my husband be surprised?

Grace sleeps heavily and her breathing is loud. How lucky for me that she drank deeply of whatever foul spirit she prefers. I creep to her cushioned rocking chair by the chimney and carefully slip the key from her apron pocket into my hand. For once, she does not stir and grip my wrist, opening her eyes and chuckling at having thwarted my escape. As silently as I can, I slide the heavy old key into the lock and twist. Yes, the door opens! But wait, there is no light! What is this blocking my way? I step back and retrieve a candle from the little table where my meals are served. Oh, I see. There is a tapestry covering the door frame. He was been cautious to keep my quarters well-hidden. I lift the woven material carefully and step out.

A faint slice of moonlight cuts across the floor. A large old-fashioned bed and a peculiar carved cabinet fill most of the room. I fumble in the dark to another door and fit the key into its lock; the key turns smoothly and I turn the knob gently. I am uncaged at last! I want only to find him and make him see me and hear my plea to return home. My heart races with excitement as I slowly make my way along the floor toward the staircase. I came up these steps long ago and have never yet been down them. The candle flickers and shadows splash the walls as I move. Down I go, one foot at a time, hoping not to be betrayed by a creaking board. It feels so strange to use stairs again. I grip the railing carefully, for I feel unsteady with this unaccustomed motion. I have reached the gallery. Everywhere frightening and forbidding eyes peer at me from portraits lining the walls. They are gruesome like him. They disapprove of me. They do not want me here. All my life I have met with jealousy. It is hardly my fault that I was made beautiful. If I had a knife, I would slash the canvases to pieces and stomp them under my feet. I will not be judged by these homely men and women in their strange clothes.

For so long I have lived in this house, but it is unknown to me. I go down another level. The air is different here—a faint trace of flowers—and a thick patterned carpet—so soft beneath my bare feet—runs the length of the hallway. Surely his bedchamber is somewhere along this passage. I shall find him, Edward Fairfax Rochester, the man I married, the man I hate. The night is quiet, but my heart beats as loudly as the clock ticking somewhere in the house. I cannot open each door, for no one must know I have left my cell. No one must turn me back from my course. How will I find him? Wait. There is a door slightly ajar. If I am careful, I can peep in and see who occupies the room. I steal to the open door and lean warily around the jamb. I cannot believe it! I cannot believe it! He lies within. I have found him so easily that it must be what Providence desires. Surely I am meant to confront him here and now.

I step inside the room and look about me. The fire has burned low at this late hour, and the room is dim. There is a rough mat by the hearth, the kind of thing a dog might sleep on. Perhaps that is how this door and not all others came to be partly open. I turn and gaze upon my husband sleeping just steps from me. I want to speak with him, but how can I expect him to listen? How can I trust him not to call for help and have me bolted back into that secret room? How unfair it is! He has a soft mattress, fine linens and a down-stuffed counterpane to combat the frigid English nights. I must make do with a sagging cot, coarse sheets, and a woolen blanket. Does he not realize how cruel that is for someone who grew up in a balmy place? Does he not consider that I miss being comfortable? Does he not think of how I long for the sun? No, of course, he does not! His heart is cold to me; it always has been. He does not care how I feel or what I suffer. He is cold! Always cold! I will warm him. I will remind him of the light and heat he denies me! He shall see!

Quickly I am at his bedside, and my candle is touching the fringed velvet drapery hanging about the massive bed. The curtains catch and still he does not stir. The flame grows and he does not move. I would like to watch his face when he wakes and knows what I have done, but I cannot stay. The smoke is becoming thicker and it chokes me. I must leave him here. I back out of the room and make my way down the hall. I will go back to my room for the time being and feign surprise when Grace tells me he is dead.

III

Tonight death brushed close to me. That foul maniac, my wife, nearly burned me alive in my bed, and now I find myself encamped on the drawing room sofa and unable to sleep further. The house is quiet as a tomb, and I have only my thoughts for company. Heaven bless and keep Miss Eyre for her wakefulness and the bravery to enter my room upon discovering smoke billowing from it! She is a rare thing indeed. So small yet brimming with enormous courage. I shall never forget my shock at being awakened in that manner. My little Jane—Miss Eyre, I should say—was quite unlike the serene governess of daytime. She was not the least bit timid as she flung more water in my direction, and her face was alight with purpose. I shall carry that image with me always.

I am relieved Miss Eyre, in her innocence, accepts the notion that Grace Poole is responsible for the fire. I would not have my unusual little governess afraid to remain at Thornfield. She must think it very odd that I allow Mrs. Poole to carry on here, but Jane Eyre is so well drilled in following orders after ten years in the spirit-crushing Lowood Institution that she is unlikely to defy my authority by pursuing her suspicions further.

In her own way Miss Eyre — no, I will call her Jane! In her own way, Jane is as much a peril to me as the menace who crept down the stairs and tried to kill me tonight. Jane stirs something in me, an interest and a hope that I had thought long dead. She stands up well to my imperious questions and sometimes harsh manner to her. Always within the bounds of propriety but never completely meek, Jane meets me as a fellow human. I dare say in her private thoughts she considers herself quite equal to me despite the vast gap between our ages and our social stations. Hers is an original mind. Granted, she has not been given access to a wide assortment of learning, nor has she had the opportunity to travel freely in England, much less the wider world. Nonetheless, she uses what she does know to its best advantage and generally achieves clarity of thought and expression far beyond the insipid and sycophantic speeches common to her sex. She is unlike any woman I have met in all my life. Her small and quiet exterior are deceptive without being deceitful; the spirit and mind within are beautiful and passionate indeed. Perhaps it is not good that I allow myself to spend so many evenings in her company. I am in danger of forgetting myself and growing overly fond of the young woman.

IV

Hellfire and damnation! I have failed. Scarcely had I settled myself in my cot before the door to my little room opened. My husband charged in and angrily awakened Grace from her stupor. He berated her for allowing me to get loose and endanger the household. Finished with his scornful tirade, he came and stood over me where I lay. He studied me coolly for a moment and then turned away without speaking. I could read nothing in his dark eyes. I wonder what revenge he will pour out on me now that he understands the full measure of my contempt for him. It is his own fault; he has only to let me go home to ensure his own safety. I would never seek his harm if he would simply let me go.

V

It being a clear day, Pilot and I walked across the fields to Carter's house for some manly conversation. Such was greatly needed after a morning highlighted by Mrs. Fairfax's lengthy consultation regarding dinner menus for the week and then Adele's warbling French ballads when her teacher granted her an hour's break. Carter was full of news of Britain's struggle with the Ashanti. In turn, I told him of my satisfaction with Adele's progress under Miss Eyre's tuition and how Thornfield felt a less oppressive place with the little governess in residence. It is possible I addressed my topic with more enthusiasm than discretion. Carter shuffled gravel with the toe of his boot, cleared his throat hesitantly and then said, "Rochester, I hope you will pardon my saying so, but I urge you to beware. You speak of this Miss Eyre in the tones of a man who cherishes a fondness he thinks no one else can see. I am certain that she is worthy of your praise, as you are a difficult man to please; nevertheless, my friend, I must beg you to keep a cool head. You are yet a married man. I know you have had your dalliances on the Continent, but conducting an affair at Thornfield with your dependent is another matter altogether. I would not see you exposed to disgrace, nor do I wish you to injure an innocent party despite good intentions on your part."

I was taken aback by Carter's directness. After his speech sank into my brain, I was a bit angry and paced about to regain my composure. Sensing something amiss between his dearest friends, Pilot went from one of us to the other and tried to engage us in a romp. I harshly ordered him away and he despondently went to lie under a chestnut tree. Standing before Carter, I opened my mouth to deny his accusations and found no words forthcoming beyond, "I do not . . . what makes you think . . . that is an absurd. . . ." The truth could not be denied. I had indeed allowed myself to develop a tender feeling for Miss Eyre beyond that of an employer appreciative of good service.

Carter was too kind to press home his advantage or mock me. He gave me a half-smile and lightly thumped me on the back. "Come now, Rochester. I spoke not to make you uncomfortable but to put you on your guard. It would not do for a man in your regrettable situation to foster an affection that cannot flourish. You cannot possibly marry while your wife survives, and we both know she is as strong as a bull. As your friend, I suggest you spend your time apart from Miss Eyre until this infatuation passes, as it certainly will. Give it a week or two and you will wonder what special qualities you ever saw in the girl."

"Aye, James. You do well to warn me. If you could discern my thoughts from a brief conversation, I shudder to imagine what ridiculous tales of my romantic tendencies the servants have embellished over their dinner night after night. Dear Mrs. Fairfax would be horrified if she suspected me of trifling with an inexperienced thing like Miss Eyre. Your advice is sound, friend; I shall practice reserve and keep myself aloof until my silly flutters stop. I would not have Miss Eyre awakened to my preference and nursing hopes that cannot become reality."

Carter seemed pleased by my decisiveness. He called Pilot to us and tossed an old India rubber ball until they both were tired. All in all, we passed a pleasant hour in his garden before he was called away to tend an injured stable boy at The Leas. Yes, it is as Carter says. This is the faintest fascination based on nothing. I have become interested in Miss Eyre merely because everyone else in the house is damnably dull or idiotic. She is not even pretty or buxom, after all. She possesses an original mind, but that is not reason enough to make fools of us both. I shall ride to the bookseller's shop at Millcote tomorrow and select some poetry and novels to keep me entertained in the evenings. My practicing solitude and self-improvement will be much better for all concerned. Let Miss Eyre amuse Mrs. Fairfax after her school day ends. No harm can come of that.

VI

After these eleven years of wandering, how odd it is to find here at Thornfield, the place I have dreaded and avoided, precisely the treasure I sought while I roved the continent. I love her. I, Edward Fairfax Rochester, love Jane Eyre. Despite the obstacles of age and position, despite the many reasons that I should not admit it, I am hopelessly smitten with my ward's governess and I cannot conceive of living without her. She is no beauty I confess, but what good have I ever found in choosing a handsome woman? Bertha, Celine, Giacinta, and Clara all were lovely in skin and bone, yet they were very ugly in behavior, nature, and cast of mind. My Jane, for she must be mine now, is their superior in every way that is important and enduring. With no conscious effort she has charmed me and won my heart.

What does it matter that I am yet a married man? How can it be wrong for me to love a woman who is my match in every fundamental? Who would be hurt if I were to marry Jane, an orphan who has spent her life without the appreciation and adoration her fine qualities deserve? Am I not as good as free? Will I not care for her tenderly if she will accept me? Can it not be that she can be both a reward and a penance, that Providence means for me to redress the wrongs of my past by treating Jane to every joy within my power while sharing in that same bliss?

Will she accept me? How am I, a man of twice her age and tarnished morals, to convince this fresh and faultless girl that I love her, that she alone has rekindled the feelings and hopes I buried long ago? Damn my stupidity for testing Jane's tolerance by explaining to her how Adele came to be at Thornfield! She knows me now as a rake and user of women. If I confess my ardor and propose marriage to her now, what will she think? Will she not suspect me of seduction at worst or mockery at best?

I do not care a fillip what the rest of mankind thinks, but I must have Jane's approval. With her at my side, I will become a better man, the kind of man I might have been had I never gone to Jamaica. Jane's innocence and goodness will help reform me. If I am fortunate enough to win her affection and confidence, I will finally cast off the shroud of bitterness that has darkened my outlook and separated me from my fellow man. I may know what it is to smile and laugh with sincerity again. If darling Jane will have me for her husband, I may in time sire sons and daughters who will know what it is to be wanted and loved by their parents. Yes, much good could come of our union. That cannot be wrong. By God, it cannot be wrong!

VII

Although I have cared little for Thornfield Hall itself, the estate—the garden, the orchard, the fields, and the tenants' cottages—always have spoken to something deep within me. It is these places that fill my mind's eye when I have been away for too long. If I had been allowed to follow my own desires after university, I believe I could have been quite happy managing the property for Father and Rowland. It is not impossible that I might have excelled at the task, increased our profits, and expanded our bounds. Even now I enjoy the sight of hay being brought in and like to go out with the men while they work. I was not meant for an idle life; I much prefer being out of doors doing something active. When I must engage in nothing but tedious amusements, I get restless as Mesrour when he has been stalled for days during the rainy season.

Father's pride—always Father's pride—stood in my way. One Christmas holiday while home from university I tried to persuade him to let me oversee our properties and try some new methods. I had convinced myself that I could spend most of my time at Ferndean Manor away from Father's disapproving gaze studying agricultural innovations—and dabbling in botany and entomology, truth be told. It seemed a pleasant and honorable way of living to me. I asked only that he grant me a very modest allowance to supplement what would come to me from my mother's inheritance. It seemed probable that the changes I proposed would more than recompense him for my stipend. My logical plan quickly was refused. Father heatedly argued that I could not be seen as a mere steward; such would damage the family name. I would not think of pursuing any course which would lower the Rochesters in the world's estimation. The discussion ended with him telling me to leave his study and stay out of his sight till the morrow. I never have understood what drove Arthur Rochester to guard our name so carefully and with more snobbery than George Osborne and Fitzwilliam Darcy together.

I was left with few choices for supporting myself, and none of them appealed to me. I would not go to the clergy, as I was repelled by the notion of sermonizing with no real enthusiasm. In my tender youth I was sincere and abhorred the idea of being a hypocrite who speaks as an avenging angel Sunday but lives as a self-serving spendthrift the other six days. Also, my father had no connections for ensuring a living he would have considered suitable.

The next obvious step would have been a commission in the army. Despite my enjoyment of an active life, I could not lean toward this path either. The thought of being ordered about by men who had bought their positions rather than earning them by merit was distasteful. I had letters from friends who had gone to the army with ample proof that living in that manner was soul-wearying despite the camaraderie in the junior officers' quarters. Again and again, one acquaintance after another bemoaned the ineptitude of his particular commander and wrote, "If only there were more men like Wellington . . . ." In any case, an officer I was not meant to be.

The life of a barrister was my last respectable career option, yet I had no heart for the law, which seemed too dry and confining to my young mind. Also, I was resistant to being required to stay in London for terms. I wanted to explore the world when and where I pleased, like every other impractical young man who pretends the money for such adventures will appear in his pockets without toil. Furthermore, I was well-aware that my personal appearance was unattractive enough without the addition of a robe and a wig. I suspected that, if ever a case gained notoriety, I would become easy fodder for the cartoonist's pen in the daily papers. Even an ugly man can be vain, you see.

Perhaps I was foolish at twenty. Perhaps I should have accepted that no career is perfect and taken my chances at building a life that offered independence from my family, if nothing else. It is hardly likely I would have been more miserable in that alternate existence. Well, who is not idealistic and uncompromising in those first years of adulthood? My own stubborn pride in the man I wanted to become prevented my becoming a curate, an officer, or a barrister; therefore, I opted to become a husband. Some part of me wanted to satisfy my father and remain a gentleman, so I took the boat to Jamaica.

VIII

I have been napping, for lying curled in my blanket is the best way to forget the cold. I awake when Grace returns with her cup and jug of porter as well as a round of Cheddar and an apple. Grace's teeth not being what they once were, she has brought a knife. I see its handle sticking out from under the napkin meant to hide it. I shall be watchful tonight. When she sets the tray on the table, I am struck by an oddity. What is this? I cannot understand why, but Grace has allowed a stranger to join us tonight. Who is this tall, slender visitor wrapped up tightly in a sealskin coat as if he were outdoors in this detestable country in a blizzard? Why has she brought him here? What does he want? No one other than Grace, the man called Carter, and that bastard Edward Rochester has ever crossed the threshold of this remote room. The man keeps his back to me and draws close to the fire, rubbing his hands together. He turns toward me and I can see his face now.

That face is so familiar. It reminds me of . . . no . . . perhaps . . . surely not . . . can it be? Richard! It is Richard! My beloved brother has come for me. Oh, my heart pounds! I scarcely can breathe. Finally, he has found me, and I shall go home. I must tell him how happy I am. The words come so quickly I cannot make sense of my own speech. I do not know which language to use. Oh, home, home! I shall go home! I want to embrace him after these many years apart; I want to share my joy. I bound toward him like a delighted child. What is this? Why does he back away? What is that look on his face? He seems frightened and on the verge of tears. Why? How could he fear me, his own sister? Why does he not greet me gladly? I have never harmed him. I always have loved him dearly. Why did he come here if not to help me? He has backed into the corner and covered his face with his hands. I cannot understand why he treats me as a monstrous stranger. Am I not Bertha Mason, his sister? Ah, I see now. Richard does not want me to come home. He wants to keep Papa's wealth for himself. There is something he does not want me to know and see in Jamaica. He wants to keep Maman's *whereabouts from me! He has been part of the conspiracy all these years! Richard, Richard, always Papa's preferred child, always more English in his ways. I still must be more like* Maman. *I must have more of her blood. What is wrong with my blood? Richard must share his good blood, his English blood. If I had more of it, perhaps I would know how to behave as they wish and be free. I could leave this room. I could leave my husband, my English husband who never cared a whit for me. If only I had more of Papa's English blood, I might be allowed to leave. Yes, that is it! Now I know what to do. I will take it. I will take Richard's blood. When I have enough of it, I will be amply*

English to satisfy them all. How simple. Before anyone can guess my intentions, I snatch the knife from Grace's tray and drive it into my brother's arm. Richard twists away from my grasp. His shirt is torn from his shoulder. His perfect blood begins to flow. How he struggles! He tries to push me away. He will not share! I will have it! I must drink his blood! I will be free! I grasp him by the throat to make him be still. Grace tugs at my arm, causing me to drop the knife, but I pay her no mind. I sink my teeth into Richard's bare arm, and he screams. He begs and calls for my husband. Damn them both! I shall not let go. I shall drain every drop of his Englishness. Grace pleads with me to stop. She tells me that I will be sorry when I know what I have done. She pulls at my arm even harder, but I merely bite down doggedly and suck the warm liquid as it oozes through my teeth. Oh, what is this? Now another person has entered the room and wrapped his arms around my waist. It must be my husband, for he is stronger than I, and this grip is merciless. Now Grace has her hands on my jaw trying to make me release Richard. Richard weeps but does nothing to free himself. Perhaps he understands now that I am doing what I must. Damn it! Grace has succeeded in prying my mouth open, and I am being dragged backwards in the direction of my cot. Grace starts toward Richard, but my husband orders her to forget "that coward" and bring the rope. I fight hard and dirty but my energy is waning. In a matter of moments, my arms are tightly bound to my sides and all I can do is flop onto my side and rain curses onto all three of them. What gives them the right? It is not my fault that the Creole blood came to me. Maman, Maman, *why do they hate us? If we are so bad, why did Papa and this Rochester choose us for wives? Why was Richard spared this indignity? He is your child, too.* Maman, *how did he escape this curse? Richard is pathetic. He is slumped in the corner sniveling loudly over a little blood. I am the one who should cry. I am the one who cannot come and go as I please. I am glad when my husband sharply tells Richard to be quiet and leads him away. I hate them both. I wish I could kill them both with my hands. Now I am crying weakly out of exhaustion and rage. Grace comes to me with a damp cloth and asks if I can be good now. I nod. She warns me to keep my teeth to myself but carefully wipes away the blood which is smeared around my mouth and down my chin. Sometimes I wonder if Grace genuinely cares for me, if she regrets her part in keeping me caged. She never could be my equal, but perhaps she could have been my friend in another place and another time. He has commanded her to leave my arms tied till it is time for breakfast, but she lifts my feet onto the mattress, saying that there is no reason for me to suffer in an awkward position for hours even if I have been a right terror. I will never hurt Grace on purpose. I must remember that.*

IX

That weak fool Richard Mason came near to ruining me last night! Any chance remark of his could have revealed what I have striven to conceal for ten years and more! What possessed him to arrive here unannounced?

Why did his long-dormant conscience drive him to make such an unpleasant journey to see his sister? Have I not kept my promise to write him with news of her? Were he not so frail, I would grind him under my boots with pleasure! No, I must not let fear make me unreasonable. I must calm myself and consider best how to get him quietly out of England.

Dick always was devoted to Bertha and to me by extension. My father-in-law has died at last and left behind the fortune he amassed shilling by shilling. Without that old despot to rule every action and thought, Dick has wasted his time and money in hopes of finding his sister improved. I pity him although he is a risk to me. The long sea voyage must have been awful for a man of his delicate constitution. How stunned he must have been to find his cherished sibling little better than a beast, and what nightmares he will suffer for the rest of his life! Yes, I must pity him, no matter how near disaster he has brought me.

Throughout my years in Jamaica, Richard Mason was my true friend. He warmed to me quickly when we first met, and I enjoyed his jovial company. He took me riding whenever we both were free and introduced me to many extraordinary indigenous plants and creatures that awed me with their vivid colors and variety. He escorted me about Spanish Town and did his best to make me comfortable among both his father's friends and our contemporaries at social gatherings and in business settings where I learned a bit about the sugar trade to prepare myself for a long stay in the tropics. As we came to know one another better, a trust developed between us and we shared much of our inner thoughts, as well as our imprecise plans for the future. Richard understood well the feeling of oppression I had experienced at my father's side and privately urged me to make the most of my freedom from Arthur Rochester's control. He knew precisely what I meant when I quoted, "*Optima ratio ulciscendi, non similem malis fiery.*" One day Richard astounded me by boldly declaring, "Damn it all, man! This is a new place and a new life for you. You shall have a new name as well. Henceforth, I shall call you Fairfax rather than Edward to mark the change. How does that suit you?" I chortled at his declaration and accepted my new appellation cheerfully. It is a pity neither of us realized one-tenth of our ambitions from that first year of companionship. In a different place and time we might have done great things, made remarkable contributions.

Occasionally, amiable Richard and I sailed out together and enjoyed a simple meal on deck after anchoring in an unclaimed cove. There we talked and laughed together as if the pressures of striving to satisfy his overbearing father and the discord in my marriage with his increasingly difficult sister did not exist. We shared a zeal for poetry and passed hours arguing mock violently about the merits of Samuel Taylor Coleridge and William Wordsworth. Inevitably, our conversation meandered from "The Rime of the Ancient Mariner" to its possible source. Time and again, we canvassed the old Bounty mutiny and the rumours that Fletcher Christian had returned to England more than once. Some days, however, we simply rested silently and exulted in the liberty of doing so.

It was Richard, during one of these day trips, who told me the truth behind the Mason facade. He said he thought it very wrong and ungentlemanly to conceal the weighty matter of his and Bertha's defective bloodline from a friend and begged my forgiveness for being part of the plan to deceive me. Of course, my tightly controlled brother-in-law revealed the facts of his mad mother and imbecile brother only after we had consumed two bottles of wine and the better part of a third. (Such excess was atypical for us, but I suspect my companion needed to pique his courage for the confession. Repeatedly that afternoon he insisted that I, his dearest, nay only, friend Fairfax, must have another glass with him to celebrate the fine day.) Later, he wept ardently with grief for his mother's wretched condition and his fears that his faculties would decay to a similar state. He was inconsolable and raved almost incomprehensibly in his anguish until he vomited over the keel. I comforted him the best I could and let him rest until he was fit to turn homeward. We never spoke of that afternoon, for I did not want him to feel shame after he had tried to do me a worthy service. Richard Mason never has been a strong man, but he has tried to be a good one. I forgave him then, and I must forgive him now.

Enough of the past—I must return to this day and its problems and rewards. Again Carter has proved himself my true friend and loyal helper. Truly, I owe him a debt for coming to my aid without hesitation or question. It is wrong that Society will not accept such a man as a gentleman simply because he uses his talents to earn his keep. Gentleman! I scoff at the notion that having the option of squandering his inheritance like Celine's *cher vicomte* or young Eshton downstairs makes one more of a gentleman than Carter. Does that belief make me a hypocrite, as so little of my own income is derived from my personal efforts? Perhaps it does, but my opinion is unchanged.

I am thankful that Carter remains a bachelor and may house Mason discreetly until the poor despairing creature is well enough to travel. Fortunately, Carter's old servant woman is half-deaf, so I need not fear her eavesdropping when Mason gushes forth his tale, as doubtless he will. My mind will not be easy until my brother-in-law is on a fast ship back to the tropics where he belongs, yet I must return my attention to entertaining the guests I have brought upon myself. One in particular must be kept occupied.

When I act the part of suitor to Miss Blanche Ingram, there are curious moments when I feel that I am reliving my courtship of Bertha. The smiles, the falsely modest lowered eyes, and the compliments that strain credulity are eerily similar at times. This sensation doubtless is heightened because the lovely Blanche bears a passing resemblance to Bertha, as she was then, in build and coloring—tall, buxom, olive skin, masses of curled black hair artfully arranged. I suspect they share much in temperament as well, although Miss Ingram dares not reveal her bad humor to me before the register book is signed. Granted, Miss Ingram has the benefit of a better education than my so-called wife, but I find she has neither depth of understanding nor thoughts of her own. She will have nothing within to sustain her when her looks fade. I foresee for her a future as a bitter gossiping spinster or a cruelly interfering mother-in-law.

If I had reason to think her pursuit of me were anything but mercenary, I would not trifle with Blanche Ingram. I would not do such a thing to Mary Ingram or one of the Eshton girls, for instance. Their hearts are tender and it would be reprehensible to wound them knowingly. La Blanche is a different sort; she intends to live in a higher sphere than the small park and shrunken fortune of her family can furnish her. She is determined to rise and stand out in society. No scruples or youthful sentimentality will block her goal. She may flirt as much as she likes while a guest at Thornfield, but I am no young, inexperienced boy to be taken in by her wiles. I have played this game before and see the trap before it can close on me this time. Perhaps I am unfair to the young woman, but I do not think it likely. When this party disbands, I will conduct a test to see how deep Miss Ingram's attachment to me runs. I will be very surprised if her ardor flourishes after it has been reported to her that the Rochester wealth is but a fraction of what she expected.

The charade I enact with Miss Ingram does not make me happy, for it pains the person dearest to me in this world. Indeed, when I happened upon Jane in the hall last night she verged on tears. I know no more effective means, however, of proving to my darling little one she alone holds my heart and all the love in it than by letting her see me reject the feminine charms and loveliness that are cast before me daily in the person of Miss Ingram. I shall repay Jane's present despondence with a lifetime of devotion. She shall be no mere mistress who fills my arms and my bed for what she can get. No, Jane will be my true wife, for are we not formed for one another? Surely no reasonable person could call the monster upstairs my wife. Ours was no real union from the beginning, and I can hardly be called married in these circumstances. Did the law but allow, I would have set her aside years ago. If she were not mad, I could have had some recourse, even if a parliamentary decree would have drained my coffers and made me an outcast. No, this way is best. It will be well; no one will be harmed. I will marry and protect Jane, who has been friendless and unloved for the better part of her life, and no one need be the wiser. Mrs. Poole's silence can be bought, and Carter will hold fast to my secret I am certain.

X

He has taken my freedom. He has kept me from my child. He keeps me caged as an animal and regards me as an animal, so I shall henceforth live as an animal. I shall crawl on the floor. I shall growl and howl and snarl. I shall let my hair hang in my face. I shall lap up my food without a spoon. I shall skulk in the dark. I shall eschew soap and water. I shall keep my shift only because this room grows frigid when Grace locks me in and allows the fire to dwindle, an unwelcome occurrence which happens more frequently of late. What point is there of behaving as a woman when no one will see me as such? What hope do I have of ever living outside of this place, of being granted liberty? I comprehend now that I likely am doomed to squander what remains of my life in this hidden room. No one who could help me knows I am here, and those who know I am here will not help me. What reason is there for me to make any attempt to be good according to their rules?

Even Grace fears me now. She, like my husband, misunderstands why I bit Richard-- why I had to do it—and thinks me a lowly savage. The warmth has gone out of her face when she looks at me. She has grown silent and cool to me in the evenings while she rocks and sews, and appraises me carefully whenever I move about to stretch my limbs. This change in her attitude makes me sad, so sad. She is not my friend after all. Her former concern for my welfare was false. She stays with me only to earn her wages. If that hateful man, my husband, were not in this house, I am certain she would lock me in day and night and abandon me altogether. I am friendless and can trust no one. If I am ever to go home, I shall have to make my own way.

XI

When I was a girl, Martine used to pamper me and spend her free hours telling me what a charming life I would have when I was grown. With my mother's looks and my father's fortune, it was a certainty that I would marry well and be very happy she said. Are all girls treated to this false dream before their nuptials? There has been nothing charming or happy about my marriage. Oh, in the early days there were superficial pleasures. Edward Rochester was besotted with me and granted my every self-indulgent request. I bought frocks, slippers, hats, and baubles as often as I liked. I ate well, had wine when I pleased, and danced often although doing so was not strictly proper after the wedding. I foolishly thought life would go on this way. I never considered that someday my husband would find me contemptible, would revolt against my every habit, would drag me from the only home and only people I had ever known and then abandon me to one bare room and one austere companion.

XII

I have told him of my plans to wed Jane and then remove her from Thornfield, and Carter is furious at me. He turned quite white as he spoke passionately about the immorality of my actions. He pleaded with me to leave Miss Eyre alone or at the very least to wait a year or two in the event that Bertha's health begins to fail. Perceiving that I cannot be dissuaded, my friend has named me a "damned, selfish fool bent upon dishonoring an innocent girl." He grew even more wrathful when I asked if his implacable disapproval meant that he promptly would expose me as a bigamist to the church and the courts. The color rushed to his face, and I thought for a moment that Carter would forcibly remove me from the premises. Thankfully, he vented his rage by striking a log in the fire with the iron poker several times. Breathing heavily, he turned and replied ardently, "For Christ's sake, man! Do you not know me at all? Have I not kept of your first marriage clandestine even when you left England for years at a time? I deplore what you are doing. I will beseech you every day to reconsider. I will not, however, be the instrument of your ruin. You have been my friend and patron many a year, and I will honor that fact even if you do not honor me by following my counsel. Rochester, it is for our Heavenly Father alone to reveal your crime and punish you if He chooses. I only can hope that you will relent. Leave my home, please. I have nothing more to say to you today." In the face of such a declaration, I could but gather up my coat and my hat and depart in silence. Never has the walk from Carter's cottage to the gates of Thornfield Hall seemed so long.

I am stung by Carter's denouncement, but I cannot expect him to understand why I must act contrary to law. His dedication to his occupation has solidified his bachelorhood. He but rarely passes time with any woman who has not suffered a sprain or some other malady. When did he last dance? When did he last chat amiably with a girl merely for the pleasure of doing so and making her smile?

If he ever had known what it is to love a compatible woman wholeheartedly and be loved in return, he perhaps would appreciate why it is worth risking even one's very soul for happiness. I will not ruin Jane; to the contrary, I will cherish her more than any man living could. I will open her eyes to a world of beauty beyond anything she has experienced in her sheltered life. She need never know about Bertha. That marriage was false; this one will be pure and true. Jane deserves this, and I do. In time, all will be well and Carter will concede that his objections were founded on nothing more than conventionality.

XIII

I was an infant when my mother died, and I know little of her. My father discouraged Rowland and me from raising questions concerning the woman who bore us. A curt response and an abrupt exit from the room were the unvarying results of our boyhood queries. Whether his uncommunicativeness stemmed from indifference to the wife he had buried or from a lingering heartache he was too proud to show, I cannot say. When I was nine, I discovered a miniature portrait of her wrapped in a handkerchief and tucked into one of my father's desk drawers beneath a map of the British Isles. I had been searching for the map, so I might plot a pirate's course and choose the best spot along the Cornish coast to bury a treasure. Instead, I unearthed something more precious to my young heart than all the gold of France, Spain and Portugal together. As a child who received little affection from anyone but a few servants who pitied my isolation at Thornfield, I had imagined how different my life would have been if my missing parent were present. I had concocted an elaborate fantasy in which my mother had survived the bout of typhus that, in reality, took her. The mother of my dreams made Thornfield Hall a warm and happy dwelling.

I still recall with perfect clarity the wonder I experienced as I held in my hand a tangible likeness on which to base my mother as I conceived her. Mounted in a lavishly carved setting of ebony and gold, the tiny watercolour portrait on ivory depicted a young woman with fair skin and large brown eyes. A pink ribbon was twisted through her dark brown hair, and her expression was hopeful and sweet. The work was fine and clear, obviously not a practicing schoolgirl's effort. It was not until I was much older that I realized my father must have spent a fair sum to have the portrait painted sometime before their marriage. I like to imagine that the gallery at Thornfield would have boasted an equally skilled, full sized view of my mother if she had lived. She would have done much to improve the grim air of the sour-faced men and women whose likenesses hang there now. Ah, my thoughts have wandered. I was thinking of finding the miniature many, many years ago. For the first time in my boyhood, I found myself coveting something that did not rightly belong to me and resolved to have it. Bold beyond reason, unafraid of the consequences should I be caught, I left the study with the miniature closed within my hand. I told no one I had it, not even Rowland. If my father ever noticed its absence or suspected me of purloining his property, he never told me. Perhaps some dormant paternal feeling in his breast stirred to life and made him aware how much I needed some part of my mother to carry with me.

How like my childish creation the woman of flesh truly was I shall never discern. What journals and letters she penned have long since disappeared—food for mice or burned to ash after her burial, I suppose. My father's unsentimental disposition would not have allowed for the creation of a shrine of mementos. Her dresses, her brushes, and most personal items were removed within days of the funeral, according to Maggie, an old servant who used to treat me to jam and bread in the kitchen when no one was present to disapprove. Even the bedroom where my mother drew her last breath was not sacrosanct. It was used for guests regularly in my childhood although there were many other chambers available.

What few facts I do have regarding my maternal relations have come to me mostly through my housekeeper, Mrs. Fairfax. Though fearful of being too familiar and often maddeningly vague in details, Mrs. Fairfax related what she knows about my mother on dull Sunday evenings when, as a means of passing time, I gently urged her to speak of her own youth and how she came to marry. She had learned the Fairfax history from her husband, now deceased ten years and more, who was a second cousin to my mother.

Elinor was the middle daughter of a household long-established in this locality. At one time the Fairfaxes held a considerable parcel of land and were among the first families of the county. Sadly, a wayward heir with a penchant for cards and high stakes had reduced the property and humbled his descendants in the last century. Still considered gentlefolk despite their diminished means, the Fairfaxes continued to mix among the gentry on special evenings several times a year. It was at a large assembly in Hay that my father met my mother. He, freshly home from Oxford and full of Madeira and punch, was taken with her shy manner and her pretty looks. He insisted upon an introduction by a mutual friend and kept her on the dance floor as much as her propriety allowed. He called upon her at home within the week, and a courtship soon formed.

Although he certainly could have looked higher for a wife, the neighborhood in general agreed that haughty Arthur Rochester could do worse than choosing Elinor Fairfax, who despite her limited resources was a young woman of good family and sweet temperament. Within three months he offered for her, and she accepted, finding nothing objectionable in her suitor and knowing that with her small dowry she was not assured of a better opportunity for marrying comfortably.

I often have wondered if my mother was happy at Thornfield. By all accounts, she was quiet and too well-bred to display any discontent, if such existed. Did Elinor regret marrying a man she had known for so short a time? Did she feel for him something more than duty and obligation, or was her acceptance a practical and resigned means of warding off spinsterhood and increasing poverty?

XIV

When I was a girl of twelve, Martine came to me one afternoon in the garden. It was a spring day, and I was watching my reflection in the ripples of a small pool. I was fascinated with the distorted image that stared back at me, but I could not bring myself to touch the cool surface, lest my companion should prove real and pull me into her strange world. Martine called my name and beckoned me to join her on a nearby seat under a pergola surrounded with the hibiscus for which our home was named. I cast one backwards glance at the familiar stranger in the water and then skipped to Martine's side. I wanted her to play marbles with me, for Richard had gone to town to visit a school friend and I was alone for once. Martine shook her kerchief-covered head and said, "No, child, this is no time for play. Your father wishes me to tell you something very important, and you must be still and quiet while I talk."

"Why does Papa not tell me himself if it is so very important, Martine?"

"Your father is feeling poorly and must keep to himself for a while. You must not bother him today. Now, sit, Miss Bertha, and let me speak my piece," she snapped impatiently. Normally, I was her pet; the use of my proper title indicated to me that Martine would tolerate no interruptions. I smoothed my skirt and sat next to her.

She resumed, "Miss Bertha, you know that your mother has not been well for a long time, do you not? You know that she is too sick to play with you and your brother or even to eat with the family anymore, yes?" I nodded. "Well, child, the doctors have told your father they cannot make her well, so she is going away. In fact, she left Hibiscus House this morning before sunrise. She did not want to wake you so early. That is why she did not come in to say goodbye."

Being a mere child, I did not comprehend why this information was delivered gravely and with regret. "Oh, so Maman *is going to visit Aunt Genevieve and Aunt Justine until she feels better? Will her fever be cured, so she can live in the big house again instead of her little cottage? Will she be gone long?"*

"No, my pet, your mother is not visiting her sisters. I wish that were the case, but it is not. Your mother, my beloved Antoinetta, is leaving this island, and she will not come back to us." I still did not comprehend Martine's meaning. I stared at Martine in confusion and was alarmed when tears escaped her deep set eyes and rolled down her cheeks. I twisted my fingers in my pinafore and bunched them into fists although I often had been warned not to rumple my clothes. My heart stung in my chest. Something was very wrong if calm and reliable Martine could not help but weep.

My little heart thumped faster than the wings of the doctor birds that frequently swooped and buzzed about the garden. In my fear I nearly shouted. "Martine! Martine! Please tell me why she must go! Is Maman *so ill that she will die? Why are you crying?"*

"Your mother is not dying, but she cannot live on this property any longer. The doctors have told your father it is not safe for her to stay with us. Without meaning to, she could do us all great harm. She cannot even stay in her little house with her nurse, Marie, now. Perhaps someday I can explain what has happened, Bertha, but you are too young now. Just know that your mother is unwell but always has loved you and your brother better than anyone in the world." Martine paused and struggled to gain control of her quivering mouth. She took my small hands into her large warm ones and spoke gently. "I am crying, my pet, because I have loved your mother since before she was your age. I was there when she was born. Not even you, my pet, were such a pretty baby. I watched her grow into a beautiful young woman. I helped her dress for her wedding and then stood by as she gave me Richard and you to love as well. I am sad that I will not see my dear girl again in this life. I am growing old, my pet, and losing Antoinetta is breaking my heart." She clasped me to her bosom and pressed her mouth to the part in my hair. Now I began to weep. I

sobbed in sympathy with my nursemaid and because I could not comprehend how I could ever be happy again without my lovely Maman. *For a very long time Martine held me and stroked my hair until I was limp with exhaustion and had no more tears to shed.*

XV

There has been much coming and going in this place the last few days. I have heard horses and the carriage several times. It is not like him to stay in this place so long, nor to be so busy. What is it that he is planning? Has he realized that I know my child is in this house, and is he preparing to remove her before I find a way to protect her? With Grace once again incapacitated by the strong-smelling drink she took after dinner, I have crept downstairs to investigate. I will not go to him tonight. I would much rather look about and try to find my daughter. Surely she is kept near him, so he may watch her carefully.

I shall try this room first. The door opens silently when I twist the knob, and I step inside cautiously. My eyes have grown accustomed to the darkened house, and I look about me in wonder. This room is small, but its walls are papered in a cheerful pattern. There was nothing dreary or shabby here, unlike my own quarters. The bed is occupied, and I must know by whom. I step nearer and examine the young woman who lies sleeping. Alas, she cannot be my daughter. Who is she then? Why has she been given a place of comfort and refuge in this house? I know my husband has no sisters, nor any near kin, so I do not know how to account for her. I move about the room hoping to find something which may explain her presence. There in the corner is a trunk already corded tightly. I peer at the label and am astounded to find that it reads, "Mrs. Jane Rochester." What can it mean? She cannot be his wife! However, there draped across the chair in front of the mirror is a mass of delicate material that can be nothing other than a bridal veil. Hanging from the armoire door is a length of shimmering white satin. The truth is clear. My husband intends to marry again.

I was a lovely bride; all of Spanish Town declared it. The same cannot be said of the plain little thing in the bed over there. What can he mean by trying to wed her? Perhaps he chooses her because she is English with nothing foreign or exotic about her. It may be that he has selected her to erase whatever traits our daughter has inherited from me. Yes, that must be it; it is just the sort of thing he would do. What he is doing is wrong! To use a word he once favoured, it is a sin. I am his wife even if he has never been the husband I wanted. How far from what I hoped for on my wedding day is the life I lead now. If only I had known . . .

I recall my wedding day. I remember the beautiful embroidery on my gown and the cool feel of pearls on my neck when Martine fastened the clasp. How pretty I was! Even Papa was proud to have me on his arm as he strode toward the altar. It is a shame for this fine, filmy veil to be wasted on a homely child like her. I shall put it on for a moment and relive my glory. There. I step forward, so I can admire my reflection. The image that greets me is terrible! It cannot be! No! What has happened to me? Can this be me in the mirror? Have I truly grown so fat and hideous? Is my hair in fact this coarse tangle? No, no! Why has he let me grow ugly? I am now as ugly as he! This would not have happened if he had let me stay in Jamaica. There I would be unchanged, attractive and desired. He did not want anyone else to love me, so he brought me to this awful place and made sure I would be changed into something horrible. That Grace must be a witch who has cast a spell to take my looks. I cannot stand the sight of myself! I tremble in disgust and rage.

This wedding apparel is a mockery to me, his real wife. Well, his little English chit shall not have this veil at least. I have ripped it past repair and scrubbed my feet upon it. She will not wear it to the church now. I have seen to that. When she cries to him about the loss, perhaps he will guess I have shown my disapproval of his wickedness.

XVI

Finally! The torturous four weeks of our engagement have ended. Under the watchful eyes of Mrs. Fairfax, Jane has proven a prickly creature since she accepted my proposal. She has evaded my caresses and returned my kisses in only the most perfunctory manner. Well, that concern for respectability soon will change. Once we are wed, passionate little Jane Rochester will welcome my embrace. Not only will I teach her all the pleasures of man and wife, but also in time I will convince her that she deserves every bit of luxury I shower upon her. Her dull, simple gowns will be replaced by sumptuous silk frocks in the loveliest hues. She will set aside her one simple brooch and allow herself to be adorned with the splendid jewels of the Rochester family. My independent wife may struggle against me at first, but some day she will allow me to hire a ladies maid to dress her and arrange her hair in the most flattering styles. Truly, I want the world to see my Jane as worthy of respect and equal to any lady of great birth.

The day has come when I will claim Jane as my wife at last. My eagerness made it difficult to sleep, yet I feel energetic. The sun has risen and there is every promise of a lovely day. All the preparations have been made, and nothing can stop me now from having that which I desire. Our trunks are packed and labeled, the wedding breakfast is being prepared now, and the new carriage stands shining in the yard. All is well. I make a vow here to myself that I shall protect, love, and provide for Jane as long as I draw breath. Every good thing I do for her will atone for the sins of my past.

PART FOUR

I

It has been a long, difficult night. Sleep has been impossible. I have paced the confines of my bedchamber for hours trying to conceive of a rational speech and incontrovertible arguments whereby to overcome Jane's naive moral objections and convince her to accept my offer to remove her forever from Thornfield and all its unpleasantness. What is immoral about an abiding love that binds two spirits such as ours? What is immoral about dedicating my every waking moment to Jane's never-ending happiness? What is immoral about showing her all the wonders of love this world can offer? My first marriage was a mockery of the vows Bertha and I made and a mistake for which I have paid a high price. Wedding someone I barely knew for reasons of convenience and security was immoral; nothing about a union with Jane ever could be so. By her own goodness she will make me good. The memory of her overwrought weeping, her pale face, and her little hands so cold in mine has torn at my heart since she left me last evening. I have felt akin to Prometheus and Sisyphus, doomed to relive that terrible scene again and again with no lessening of pain. Oh, I long fervently for sunrise, so that I might go to her room decently and reassure her that my love will remain unchanged and eternal even without the benefit of a formal blessing from people who know nothing of us. Have each of us not earned the right to bliss by enduring loss and suffering from our earliest days—she at Gateshead and I here at

Thornfield? Our fidelity to one another for the rest of our lives will make all right regardless of what some fusty law books or hypocritical clerics may say.

I never shall forgive Mason for his interference yesterday. He, of all people, should sympathise with the wrongs I endured at the hands of our fathers and his sister. Did he not witness Bertha's mania at its worst when he intruded upon Thornfield Hall? Was not his very blood spilled by the creature he purports to be my rightful wife? By God, if I had had any reasonable alternative, I would have turned Grace Poole out the very next day for accepting Mason's bribe and taking him to see his most loving sister! Had Mrs. Poole not betrayed me for a few coins, the disastrous interruption yesterday might never have come to pass. What of John Eyre? Who is this unknown and absent uncle to intrude on his niece's wedding day?

I partially open the blinds and find that the sky has faded from black to pale gray. Soon the sun will shoulder its way over the horizon. Hasten yourself, fiery ball! I will not sing an aubade this day! I burn to see my darling girl and be assured that she has not sunk into despair over what she must mistakenly believe to be our broken future and her own shame. However, I must strive for patience and allow Jane to lie abed for as long as she likes this morning, as yesterday's trials must have fatigued her frail body to its limit. Sleep will both do her well bodily and calm her agitated spirit. Yes, today will be better for both of us. Having replenished her strength and cleared her acute mind, Jane most certainly will listen to my plans dispassionately today and approve them. She will help me choose our path to the Continent and share my eagerness to be gone from England and its rigid conventions. Yes, she will welcome the freedom and the change. She was only surprised and embarrassed yesterday after the abrupt disruption at the altar. What young woman would not have been distressed at such a confounded scene? Having had time to consider what I told her of my first marriage, having come face to face with the monster upstairs, my sensible Jane will consult her own knowledge of my character and follow her heart. There can be no other conclusion.

♦

The blood surges wildly in my veins and I can wait no longer! Moments ago the clock struck nine, yet Jane has not emerged from her little room. She must have awakened by now, even if I did order everyone in this house—and especially noisome Sophie and Adele— in strictest terms to stay hushed and far clear of Jane's room until she is ready to arise. I fear that passionate and worried little Jane has become feverish and is lying ill and too weak to summon assistance. I recall now that she ate almost nothing and had but a glass of wine to slake her thirst all day. Furthermore, she was near to fainting yesterday afternoon. It is quite possible she ails and is too proud to summon me, and I cannot bear the thought of her suffering. I will delay no more. No matter how improper Mrs. Fairfax finds my actions and no matter how she protests, she will agree that she is in my service and must hand over the keys when the master of the house demands them. Prudishness has no place here! If Jane is unable to come out of her own accord, I shall enter her room and see that she has the tenderest care. If she is unwell, I shall bathe her brow and give her broth by the spoonful. I shall support her better than any pile of feather pillows and talk to her quietly until she is cheered.

♦

Never have I been a patient man, but Mrs. Fairfax's attempts to dissuade me from entering Jane's room at all raised my ire. It may be some time before my housekeeper forgives me for speaking to her so harshly. Still, I cannot consider a silly old woman's hurt feelings when my dear girl needs me. Finding it on the bulky ring, I carefully fit the key into the lock and prepare to turn it quietly, not wanting to jar Jane's nerves if she has lapsed back into sleep. To my astonishment, I discover the door never was locked. I try the sturdy latch and it rises without resistance. Puzzled and troubled, I thrust the door wide and look inside the small compartment that has been Jane's since she arrived at Thornfield Hall. (She never could be persuaded to transfer to a larger and finer chamber after we became engaged. She insisted that she would be "quite uncomfortable amidst all that superfluous comfort.") My eyes scan the room again.

The bed is made, and Jane is not here. How odd! I cannot fathom why she did not come to me immediately upon dressing. She must know that we have much to discuss before we begin our journey. Moreover, she knows my nature well enough to guess at my impatience to see her.

Ah, well. I must make allowances. This is provoking, self-reliant Jane. She must have wished for some solitude to start her day and craftily managed to slip past my door without a sound. (I must admit her ability to do just that has proven useful more than once this past year.) Undoubtedly, I shall find my little fairy in the garden, strolling among the flowers to stretch her restless limbs or sitting on our bench and enjoying the fresh morning air before she breaks her fast. She was pent up in one room for nearly the whole day when we returned from the church, so she must have wanted the pleasures of nature.

Alas, Jane is not in the garden after all. My walk there resulted in nothing more than damp boots. Where is she? What can she mean by leaving the grounds? I am peeved but must not become angry with her. It is quite possible that she has walked into Hay to post a letter. Perhaps she has penned her meddling uncle an explanation of how she will not accede to his expectations and leave my side, as I am the one man with whom she could exist in perfect harmony and mutual understanding. I must not fret. She will return soon and all will be well.

♦

I have tried to occupy myself with reading, but that has been a fruitless task. Time after time, I had to read a page over twice or thrice, having been distracted by my inner thoughts or sounds that I hoped marked the advent of my beloved's return. Instead, I have found only that I cannot abide Mrs. Radcliffe and that Leah is easily startled by doors flung open suddenly. It is noon and still Jane does not appear. My anxiety will not be stilled. Where is the woman? Does she think nothing of how I ache to see her? She must be hungry, so why does she stay away? Rochester, think, man! If she walked to Hay, she will be famished, so she very likely stopped in at Mrs. Thompson's shop to have some tea and a bun or two before strolling homeward. She is too practical to starve herself all morning and then risk turning homeward only to swoon into a hedgerow because of hunger. At any time now, she will come tripping up the gravel path, her elfin face brightened by the sun and exercise. There will be no use in remonstrating with her, for she will be guided by her own desires in these small matters.

♦

An hour ago I rode out astride Mesrour with Pilot running alongside. I fully expected to find Jane dallying among the lanes. I was convinced she might wish to see me privately away from the house, so we could talk without eavesdroppers or the solemn disapproval of Mrs. Fairfax dampening our happy mood. Alternatively, I thought she might have turned an ankle while walking home and then been forced to sit until aid came her way. My thoughts turned to our first meeting and I was amused by how droll it would be to assist her this time. I thought of how I would rally her for having to depend on me to see her home. Strangely, Jane was not to be found anywhere along the road to Hay. I had made my way to the village and learned that she had not been spotted nearby. I turned back to Thornfield in hopes that she had beat me home by cutting across a stile or fording a brook but was disappointed yet again. Still she does not come! The sun has begun its decline and Jane remains absent. I grow worried and a more than little angry.

I have inspected the contents of her room more closely and discerned that nothing is missing from Jane's belongings other than the simple bonnet which so horrifies Adele and Sophie with their Parisian fashion sense, a light shawl, and a small purse. Surely that must mean she merely has gone for a visit to some friend she has neglected or perhaps taken the coach to Millcote for some mysterious reason of her own. After all, this is the same creature who avowed she had no family and then was absent for a month when Mrs. Reed died. Who knows what local spinster or lonely young wife she has met and become attached to without my knowledge?

♦

Darkness has fallen and Jane is yet gone. My worry grows and a shapeless fear gnaws at me. Even at her most mischievous and headstrong, Jane would not think of making an overnight stay somewhere without informing Mrs. Fairfax or at the very least leaving an explanatory note. I have called Leah, who is responsible for gathering clothing to be laundered, into Jane's room and asked her to examine the drawers and wardrobe and tell me if anything is missing. At first the housemaid quibbles about how Miss Eyre until recently has had but a few personal items. Under my stern gaze, Leah ultimately followed my orders and counted the linen and the dresses belonging to Jane. Leah's account showed that indeed there were some undergarments absent. What can that mean? Why would Jane have taken just a few things and not packed a proper trunk if she meant to travel? Why would she have left behind all the lovely wedding trousseau as yet unworn? I do not understand. Where is she? Why does she not come to me? What impulse drove her away unannounced? Jane, Jane, what have you done and where have you gone?

♦

My head is afire. I have passed a second sleepless night in ceaseless worry. All the household were questioned closely last night on pain of dismissal if I detected any mistruths, and not one of them admitted to having knowledge of Jane's departure or her current whereabouts. It is true? Has the daring little fool in fact run away with nothing but the clothing she wore? She cannot have much money, for I am her sole source of income and I have not paid her since last quarter. Ever the upright governess, Jane fiercely and repeatedly has declined to accept a shilling over her salary until after our marriage. The strand of pearls that was my wedding present lies untouched on the bureau. Even the tiny brooch she dons for special occasions is still here. So, with no belongings of worth and no ready coin, how does she expect to manage? Where does she intend to go? Where will she shelter? More importantly, why did she go at all? Aside from gossip, there is nothing to harm her at Thornfield, and soon enough we would have left all that nonsense at our backs. What impulse sent her sneaking away in the night?

I should be quite angry with my self-sufficient little Jane. A few lines laying out her planned destination and return could have been hastily scratched and saved the whole household much worry. It is unlike her to be inconsiderate, so her motives must have been strong for her to commit such a breach. I can tell Mrs. Fairfax is deeply concerned for Jane's well-being by her silence and monosyllabic replies to my questions and instructions;

indeed, she borders on discourteous in her fretful distraction. Also, I suspect my distant relation has grasped at last my relationship to the unseen tenant of the third floor. Her pious pride in the Fairfax name must be wounded. Adele, for her part, cannot be in the same room with me without lambasting me with dozens of questions about why Jane remains Miss Eyre instead of Mrs. Rochester and where she has gone. At one point, the silly child earnestly asked if I had sent Jane to the moon, as we had jokingly discussed during a recent carriage ride to buy clothing for Jane. Ultimately, I have had to order Sophie to keep Adele out of my way. I have worries enough without being harangued by Celine Varens's bastard.

Jane, if only I knew what you were thinking, what it is you fear or abhor, I could begin to clear all obstacles. Why did you not come to me and tell me you wished for a brief respite in which to recover from the surprise of

Bertha's existence? Having you out of my sight is a trial, but I would have accepted your request so long as I knew you would come home within a few days. Never would I hold you against your will. Ha! Again Bertha Mason stands in my way. Does not her presence at Thornfield Hall contradict me? The situations are very different, however. Bertha must be confined for the safety of the household. Jane herself has witnessed the maniac's handiwork and would concur if pressed for an opinion.

What if I am addressing her absence in the wrong manner? What if Jane did mean to walk only to Hay and back but was intercepted and taken away by some villain? For all her spirit, she has not the strength to fend off a determined adversary. Oh, God! What if she is in some dreadful place being harmed or dishonored? Should I go to Sir George Lynn and insist that he raise an alarm to search the neighborhood? What if she has been taken farther afield? Every moment gives her abductor the advantage. I must act, but I do not know which course is best. Wait! What if she has been lured away by Mason and Briggs and they mean to abduct her to Madeira at her uncle's insistence? That could explain why she took no baggage. Clearly, she did not expect to be gone from Thornfield for long and now is thinking of how to make good her escape and return to me. Men will do much for money, and it is possible Mr. John Eyre—misled by Richard Mason's biased intelligence of my life—has laid out a large sum to secure his niece's kidnapping.

Oh, if only I knew which way to turn . . . I need reliable counsel but who can give it? Carter? Would he give me succor, or would he glory in my failure after I disregarded his many admonishments not to go through with a wedding? I do not know whom I can trust with helping me recover Jane. I wish to avoid having my private affairs opened to the gaze of everyone in the county. On the other hand, I need to cast the net wide if I am to find my dear girl.

♦

Jane! Jane! I would not have left you in this way! Your desertion is most unkind and painful to one who adores you as I do! I must think. I must decide what to do. How can I rest until I have found you and been assured that you love me still? Yes, you do love me still. Of that I am confident. Not even the cessation of your heart's beating could bring your love for me to an end. So it is for me, and so it must be for you. We are bound together for eternity, not by some archaic promises and a gold band, but by the essence of our very beings.

II

My husband did not get his little English bride after all. He brought her to my room with others one morning. Before all present he wrathfully claimed me as his wife. According to Grace, who forgot her customary reserve and gossiped shamelessly about my husband's passion for his governess, this girl, his beloved Jane, fled him in the night. He cannot find her and his despair grows deeper every day. I do not pity him. Indeed, I hate him more than ever. In his anguish he has sent my child from this house, and there was little hope that I shall ever find her. I want to hurt him. I want to destroy all that is left to him.

Grace has grown careless. There was a time when she neither turned her back to me nor let me move out of her sight. Now, she has grown too fond of her porter and gin, which have dulled her senses and slowed her reactions. It was unwise of her to leave the iron by the fire when she finished pressing the handkerchiefs she embellished today, but it provides a perfect opportunity for me. Before she has time to suspect my motives, I snatch up the iron and strike her from behind. I unlock the door, grab a candle from the table, and set about my plan.

I hurry down the staircase and enter the departed governess's bedchamber. My husband burns for her in a way that he never did for me, and now I shall burn all traces of her from his life.

♦

It is done. The flames leap at my bare feet and kiss the hem of my gown. I am warm at last, but I must not ignore the danger. I flee up the stairs onto the leads. I have wanted to be in the open air for longer than I can recall. At last I am under the night sky and filling my lungs with cool, fresh air. I could dance with joy! I am free! But wait! Something is not right here. An orange glow and smoke trickle through the open door to the roof. How odd! I thought I closed it. No! No! My husband has followed me, and he is calling my name, pleading with me to come away while there is time. Why has he come?

Has he not hated me nearly half our lives? Has he not stripped me of my daughter and every reason to live? I have escaped the prison of his home. I have set it afire. He cannot put me back into that horrible room. I will not let him hold me again. I will not. I will fly away home. I will leap into the night and ride the winds home. In the morning I will breakfast on mango and papaya and pick fragrant flowers in Papa's garden. I will find Maman. *She will be pleased to see me. I will be happy again. Yes, just one more step and I will go home. Just one more step . . .*

III

God, why have you spared me? What reason have I to live a minute more? My precious Jane has left me without a word, and I cannot trace her anywhere. I am blind and crippled by the loss of my right hand. Thornfield, my home such as it was, is destroyed along with many family heirlooms. The secret of my marriage has been exposed and, no doubt, is discussed with relish in every tavern within twenty miles. Even the madwoman who was my wife is dead—a fact that should bring me relief but does not. I am rid of her at last, but it is too late. If I did wrong, and I say if, for I do not believe it so very wrong to want to be happy and make my most beloved happy . . . . If I deserved punishment, why did you not strike me down once and for all? What kind of existence is left for me? This world holds nothing of hope and peace for me without Jane. It would have been better for me if I had died among the smoking embers of Thornfield.

Most of the people and comforts I took for granted several months ago are gone. Mrs. Fairfax, shaken by the fire and what she perceives as my dishonorable attempt to marry Jane, I have granted an annuity and sent to live with friends who have retired to Bath. Adele is boarding at a school for girls, from which she writes letters that remain unopened, as there is no one here to read her French scrawling to me. Sophie, no longer required, has returned to her homeland. Leah's mother was shocked that she had worked for a reprobate and insisted that my maid resign her place with me. Grace Poole has returned to her son's home near the Grimsby Retreat. Mesrour has been sold, as I can no longer ride and being penned endlessly would be cruel to an animal of his spirit. My favourite chair, my best clothing, the leather-bound volumes I absorbed eagerly in my youth, even the cherished miniature of my mother—all are lost to me.

Partly from necessity and partly from a wish for privacy, I have taken up residence at the family's lesser house, Ferndean Manor, which is remote enough to keep me safe from the curious. I could not bear the thought of letting another property near Hay, for the inevitable visits from morally superior neighbors coming to gawk at the chastened sinner under the ostensible guise of offering sympathy would have been insupportable. The world may believe me shamed, but I do not have to display myself to them. I will not be an object of pity!

Only faithful Pilot stays with me out of love, and he must keep his distance lest I trod on his toes or stumble over him in my sightless staggering from one room to the next. John and Mary have remained out of loyalty to a man who no longer exists. Fortunately, my income has been untouched by the loss of Thornfield, so I have been able to raise their wages as compensation for being removed from their acquaintances. My old friend Carter rides over every other week; to him I must be a case to be studied and cured. Oh, how did my wretched life come to this? Is there some way I could have foreseen and forestalled the misery that has befallen me?

Jane. Jane. Unique and darling Jane. Stubborn, little Jane. I should have known her pious upbringing under the guidance of Reverend Brocklehurst would close her mind against my bargain. She may not have admired the man, but the Lowood influence is with her yet. So determined to be within the law of man and God, even if it means that she will be lonely and unloved. I am certain she cannot be happy without me. We are connected; we are made for one another. She must ache every moment as I do. I cannot understand why she felt compelled to flee as she did. How could she think I ever would do her harm? Did she not realize I never would have forced myself upon her? I gladly would have waited for her to choose the time and the place when we were united in heart and body. Oh, Jane, foolish girl, you might have at least taken something of value to aid you in whatever journey you have undertaken. Thinking that you might be hungry or settled with inferior company pains me. Why did you go? Where are you now? If you needed time to quiet your mind and decide, you had only to say so. Are you thinking of me? Will you ever return? Nay, I pray that you do not, for the Edward Rochester you knew is no more. In his place is a disgraced, tired cripple. I would not like her me to see me thus.

♦

The red glow where there should have been none first alerted me to danger the night Thornfield burned. Unable to sleep, I was roving about the house long after the servants and Mrs. Fairfax had sought their beds. Even Pilot had grown weary and left me to my solitary restlessness. That day I had received another fruitless report concerning Jane. My agents had sought everywhere they could conceive of a young lady going and had found no sign of my missing love. I bitterly reflected that imagining Jane would behave like any other being had been their mistake. I was lonely and dispirited—and a little angry with my beloved fugitive—when I made my way from the library toward my bedchamber. I had tried history, philosophy, the Greats and Mr. Thackeray, but no reading had drawn my thoughts away from my present anguish and soothed me. I was beginning to feel as one of Byron's haunted heroes destined to regret the past, Manfred in the flesh.

I moved quickly down the passageway and realized that the light was coming from the small bedroom that had been Jane's. My heart leapt when I thought for the briefest moment that she had come back to me. When I pushed the door all the way open I was met with a rush of hot air and seething flames. Evidently the conflagration has started in the bed and was spreading rapidly. Without time to consider how the fire had started, I began to rouse the house. I pounded on Mrs. Fairfax's door and barely gave her time to open it herself before informing her of the danger. I sent her to wake Adele and Sophie, while I raced up the stairs and yelled for John to come at once. Much befuddled, John answered my summons and made every effort to arrest the flames with me. With the house so spread out and the chief water supply too far from the living quarters, we stood no chance in saving Thornfield. Soon it was clear that all we could do was usher other residents to safety. John gathered Sophie, Adele, Mary, Leah and Mrs. Fairfax and hurried them across the drive and well clear of the house. With the others accounted for, I turned my attention to the attic and the two women who had not yet appeared despite the considerable commotion below. I now thought it probable that I knew how this disaster had come into being. When I entered the chamber, I found Mrs. Poole slumped in her chair and unconscious at the small deal table in the center of the room. A trickle of blood ran down the back of her neck. The maniac, Bertha Mason, was not there. When I shook her hard, Mrs. Poole moaned quietly and I was relieved that she had not been murdered outright. I suspect my wife had taken advantage of Mrs. Poole's fondness for porter and struck her unawares while she was in a stupor. As hastily as I could move with a stout and semiconscious woman in my arms, I took Mrs. Poole down the stairs and out into the cool night air. Brushing aside the party's shocked exclamations and questions, I turned back toward the house once I had been relieved of my burden. There was one more inmate to be rescued—no matter how little she might desire it. Thornfield Hall was fully alight now. When I looked skyward, I glimpsed something unexpected. Standing on the leads was Bertha, distinct against the sky in her white shift.

Whether she was seeking to escape the conflagration she had caused or just running rampant, I could not guess. It did not matter. I could not and would not leave her there to die. I drew upon my reserves and found the strength to make another trip into the blazing building. With every moment the risk grew greater; however, my conscience, my infernal conscience, demanded that I make every effort to bring my wife to safety. Whatever she had done and whatever unhappiness she brought in my life, she remained my responsibility, and even an antipathy built upon years of mutual hatred would not cause me to abandon her to an unspeakable death. Slowed by sparks and smoke from every direction, it was some time before I arrived on the third floor and felt my way to the door giving access to the roof. With some relief I dove into the fresh air and filled my lungs. I saw that Bertha had moved to the very edge of the roof and was resting between battlements. At any moment she could fall. I called to her. She turned and looked at me with dismay. I called her name again and urged her to come forward toward me. Ever determined to thwart me in my desires, she shook her shaggy locks out like a cape around her shoulders. With a single scream that seemed to me to have been, “Home!," she leapt.

♦

Shocked by what Bertha had done, I numbly descended the stairs connecting the roof and the attic and struggled toward the ground level of Thornfield Hall. I scarcely could draw breath in the polluted air, and visibility was practically nil. I made my way by gripping the banister and forcing one foot after another down each step. There were only three or four steps to go and I thought safety was within reach. I was wrong. With a mighty crash and a huge rush of flames, the great staircase collapsed and took me with it. After landing hard and having the breath knocked from me, I lost consciousness where I lay covered with debris in the darkness.

Some hours later I regained my faculties and found myself an altered man. At first I knew only that I could not see, but I assumed that had to do with the bandages which Carter had wrapped around my head. Next I became aware of the frightful sensation from my left arm. There was a horrible ache, and I could not understand. Uncertain, disbelieving, I slid the fingers of my right hand down my left shoulder and elbow into the clump of bandages that held *nothing.* In a nightmarish moment I realized that my left hand was gone—not broken, not merely mangled, but gone forever. Carter says that never in his professional life has he been so alarmed as when he heard my cry upon this horrific discovery. He had great difficulty in calming me. He at last resorted to having me held by John and the faithful men who had helped transport me to Carter's home and then waited for news of my condition. A large dose of laudanum was forced down my throat. With the horrible realization that I had once watched as the same was done to Bertha, I was equally unable to resist. I fell into an unwilling sleep, and my dreams were something dreadful. I was shackled in a hellish place, each limb stretched to its furthest extent and pinioned to the ground. The flickering landscape was populated with demons brandishing torches which they used to set me afire. Meanwhile, Jane, my mother, and old Maggie the maid of my youth battled to extinguish the flames that strove to consume me. Every time my preservers had nearly succeeded, a fresh band of demons arrived and overwhelmed them. Again and again through the night I was set aflame and tortured.

♦

Thankfully after what seemed like years of anguish I awoke to a clearer mind and the spartan furnishings of Carter's spare bedroom, where I vaguely recollected being carried the previous night. I lay still and tried to collect my thoughts, desperate to make sense of all that had happened to me. Shortly thereafter, Carter tapped at the door, called my name, and then entered. I heard him draw a wooden chair nearer the small bed where I lay. He expressed his relief that I had managed to shake off the laudanum–induced terrors of the night. Calmly and quietly he explained to me how I had been pulled from the wreckage of Thornfield Hall by tenants of the estate. By the time he had arrived, I had lost a significant amount of blood and was in danger of losing my life. With no family around him to make the decision, Carter, as my friend, chose to save me by amputating my irreparably damaged left hand. It was the best he could do, for one eye was damaged beyond hope. Carter assures me that someday I may yet regain my sight in my remaining eye, but I am skeptical. He is an honest man, but I wonder if his guilt over making the choice to remove my hand has influenced him to offer me a better future which he cannot guarantee.

After a spell of quiet reflection, I was able to set aside my own injuries and inquire about Bertha, that poor, deranged creature. Carter gently told me that she had been killed instantly and mercifully when she dropped onto the cobblestones in front of Thornfield. Her skull had shattered and brain matter was visible amidst the blood that pooled around her mangled corpse. The merest glance had assured him that she was beyond help and he had turned his professional attention to me. Carter spared me the obvious question: why had she done it? Long aware of her mental state, he was unsurprised that she had met her end thus.

After hearing a convoluted report from a witness's wife's younger brother, the magistrate had come to Carter to learn the identity of the strange woman who had died and his medical opinion of the cause of death. Loyal beyond my desserts and wishing to lighten my woeful burden, Carter informed the magistrate that the victim was a ward of the Rochester family who had long been ill. Obviously, the strain of the fire had devastated her already fragile nerves and driven her to the roof instead of down the stairs to safety. Carter did his best to urge discretion and compassion since I, tossing about in drug-fueled nightmares, was not yet in a rational state. He made every assurance that Bertha had met her death by misadventure rather than by intentional harm. Fortunately, Carter's good name and earnest appeals held sway and an inquest was found to be unnecessary. Not even Mrs. Fairfax or the servants were questioned about the fire and the circumstances around it.

It was not until some days later that the truth of Bertha's relationship to me trickled out into the public domain. Whether the story came from Leah and her family or from Mrs. Poole after someone plied her with a bottle of gin I cannot say. In either case it does not matter. Jane has fled and I shall withdraw from society. What does it matter to me now if my reputation has been damaged and I have become a pariah?

IV

My metaphysical heart may be wounded most cruelly; however, its physical counterpart beats soundly enough. As Samson before me, I have lost my power and my dignity and am disgraced before the world, but I find myself unwilling to die quietly. The will to survive is tenacious even when there are few reasons for doing so. Food may turn to ash in my mouth, but I must eat it. Water may do nothing to quench my thirst for knowledge of Jane, but I must drink it. Sleep may be a nightly torment of relived mistakes and ghastly alternate scenarios, but I must lay my head down and let it come. I cannot bear to leave this world without knowing what has become of my dear girl. The slightest potential, the faintest hope, of reuniting with her someday fuels my flesh and my spirit. Until I am certain that she has departed from mortal existence for eternity, I must live on and await her return.

I slowly am learning to live in a new way. My sight and my left hand are gone and with them countless little actions I once took for granted. At times the enormity of the trials I face in becoming more independent overwhelms me with self-pity and gloom. There have been days when my soul has been as dark as that world around me and I have wondered if indeed I have been justly punished for my sins. Some might mistake my injuries as the harshest chastisement I have received. To me, no loss is more difficult to bear than that of my little Jane, who is ever present in my thoughts. I am maddened with not knowing where she is, how she fares, if she lives at all. Unquestionably, her hardy spirit would reject any notion of self-annihilation; nonetheless, without money and someone to protect her, she is vulnerable in many ways. I cannot bear to contemplate the number of illnesses and mishaps that could befall her, the wretched company poverty may force her to keep. Thinking of her now draws my remaining fingers involuntarily to the pearls, my wedding gift to her, fastened under my cravat. I wish anew she had taken them when she departed Thornfield. Pawned, they would have kept her fed and comfortable for quite some time. I find myself beseeching God to keep her safe wherever she may be. I, a mere damaged mortal, attempt to bargain with my Maker on her behalf. I ask nothing for myself.

Throughout my life I have been proud of my strength and my grace, for they counterbalanced my decided lack of pulchritude. At leisure with my friends when no women were about, physical skill was more valuable than handsomeness, and I had that asset in abundance. That pride has fled me. Now, I have been brought low indeed. I, who once rode without fear, swam well, boxed without disgrace and fenced with distinction, am reduced to having my servant button my shirt and trousers and tie my cravat each morning. I may at least take satisfaction in knowing that John does not dress me gaudily or in mismatched clothing like some gypsy or entertainer at a country fair, for my wardrobe is all newly sewn and quite plain—a commission Carter's housekeeper was kind enough to accept when it became obvious that I could not live the rest of my days in her master's spare nightshirt and dressing gown. I would not hear of having a local tailor brought in to outfit me; instead, Carter was sent to the drapers with measurements and specific instructions on the fabrics needed. I was forced to submit to the ministrations of a cobbler since my surviving boots were ruined as I lay among the wreckage of my ancestral home, but owing to a service Carter had performed for him recently the man came to me to trace his patterns. Between the efforts of old Mrs. Davis and Mary—who called upon me when I was well enough to receive visitors and demanded to do her share of the sewing—I soon had enough simple clothing to suffice for a life of retirement. With that necessity supplied, I began making preparations for the move to Ferndean Manor.

Relocating roughly one hundred miles was no small feat. There was a time when I would have relished the list-making and bustle required for such a venture, but—wounded in body and spirit—I took on the operation as a necessity only, an escape from the judgment of the neighborhood. Indeed, the only farewell visit I requested before decamping from Carter's abode was from Mr. Pennington, who for years had functioned as a steward while I roved Europe. Assured that he would watch over my property and report any difficulties in person—the reading of letters being an impossibility—I tried to blot thoughts of Thornfield Hall from my mind and set about my tasks.

In my young adulthood I had thought to establish myself at Ferndean Manor as a means of dodging my father's ubiquitous criticism. Now, I recognized how impractical I had been in my youth, for adapting a former hunting lodge into a full-time residence was no simple matter. Every aspect of the house, its contents, and its environs had to be considered. Dispirited and sightless I was in those difficult and lonely days; however, I could not leave all decisions to John and Mary or even Carter, who assisted with the process whenever his freedom from practicing surgery and my inclination to accept his counsel allowed.

First, the roof, the chimneys, the timber beams, and the interior plaster all had to be inspected by a Lancashire builder of good reputation in order to guarantee the house would be habitable year-round. I was fortunate that a manor house so rarely occupied needed only some improved fixtures for the kitchen and a few minor indoor repairs—and a borrowed family of cats to decimate the rodent population, which swarmed about as freely as the Gauls before the legions arrived. Next, a bevy of local women—glad for the wages and curious about Ferndean and its owner—descended on the ancient place to sweep away massive cobwebs, scrub floors, wash windows, polish wainscoting, air feather mattresses, beat rugs, and perform a multitude of other chores to bring Ferndean Manor back to a livable state.

Meanwhile, workers were hired to clear the old well, dig a new privy, and lay in a supply of wood for fires. The small old stable was the only part of the property not treated to a full refurbishment. Pilot could sleep there if he wished, but we would have no horses beyond a visitor's mount, which could be stalled and fed when the time came. With the essentials of shelter in place, food and home comforts were tackled next. A gardener from Thornfield Hall was dispatched to render the small yard manageable, put in a kitchen garden, and plant a few fruit trees for seasons to come.

Mary and John traveled to Ferndean to survey what household goods would have to be bought, with so few items surviving the blaze that changed all our lives radically. Without a senior servant such as Mrs. Fairfax to direct them, my future companions and caretakers were nervous about being given the responsibility to choose the vast assortment of supplies we would find necessary, but more often than not I moodily shook off their anxious inquiries and suggestions with an oft-repeated pronouncement: "Buy what you like. Spend what you like. I do not care. For Heaven's sake, do not bother me today." Since only the three of us were to live there, the furniture already in place was adequate although one bedroom suite had to be shifted to a large chamber on the ground floor, it having been decided that my attempting to go up and downstairs would be folly. Adequate bedding, proper cookware, candles, china, and countless other sundries were organized, as well as the stocking of the larder. A local laundress was procured, and arrangements were made with a butcher and a dairyman. Also, a second maid was engaged to come weekly to help Mary with the cleaning and in the kitchen as needed.

All the while I was master of a great house, I had thought rarely, if ever, of all the people and skills that were necessary to make my household run smoothly. Now that I no longer could dash in and out when I pleased and expect my every whim placed before someone else's convenience, I marveled at the work that went on daily and without comment. I realized how abominably inconsiderate I had been to Mrs. Fairfax with my abrupt arrivals and departures through the years and how I must have upset her peace before she learned to anticipate my thoughtless habits.

V

In the early days of my residence at Ferndean Manor, I resolved to grow a beard since I could no longer keep clean-shaven on my own. A ceaseless itch—undoubtedly the work of a Deity who was not finished humbling his profligate and headstrong child—forced me to solicit Carter, during one of his flying visits to my new abode, to act as my barber. His response was a polite "Of course, Rochester, nothing could be simpler. I shall ring for John or Mary to bring warm water, soap, and a razor," but I detected a stifled chuckle in his speech and demanded to know what he found so damned amusing about my current appearance. He riposted that I would make a fine model for an artist illustrating tales by the Brothers Grimm. I muttered *sotto voce* about friends who think themselves witty and take advantage of one's inability to kick them down the stairs as they deserved. All the same, I willingly and gratefully allowed Carter to scrape my face smooth and relieve my irritated skin.

Since that day John has arrived each morning and shaved me in front of the fire in my room as a precursor to helping me dress. He neither asked for my permission to cede the ritual to him nor waited for me to request his assistance; he merely came in and said, “Sir, I have brought the water for your shave. Will you sit up in bed, or do you prefer to move over to the wing chair?” I believe he does so because this small rite is something he *can* do for me. He cannot restore my vision. He cannot replace my missing limb. He cannot ease the pain and loss that fill my heart. He can, however, keep me looking as much like the man I once was as I will allow.

What we shall do about my hair in the future I do not know. Allowing anyone else to comb it is a barrier I am not yet prepared to break. I do my best to smooth my unkempt mane by feel but know I certainly must seem a frightful creature now—a metamorphosing kinsman of dear Pilot perhaps or one of the fantastical beings about which I used to tease Jane. My locks grow wilder by the week, but I have no desire to present myself at the nearest town to have someone experienced trim it. My lingering vanity still revolts against playing the local oddity in public, and I will make do until John or Carter finds me utterly repellent and decides to act.

Depending upon others for my appearance is not the worst of my new invalid limitations. More often than not, for the ostensible reasons of having no guests to entertain and not wanting to trouble Mary with providing me a separate meal, I request stew or soup for my dinner. In actuality, I wish to avoid the embarrassment of asking Mary to cut up the meat and explain what accompanies it when she sets my plate before me. Almost daily I knock over glasses of water, goblets of wine and cups of tea. John and Mary keep to the custom of having their meals in the kitchen while I eat alone. For that I am grateful because they are not witnesses to my inevitable spills and misses. They are a loyal, decent couple who never seem aggrieved by all the extra wiping up of puddles and replacing of table linens my blind and crippled state must cause them.

John has been with my family since I was a young boy, and occasionally he lets slip a "Mr. Edward" when he speaks with me. It pains me to know that he must safeguard me in my infirmity rather than vice versa. I find it difficult to express my gratitude but hope my reliable dependents understand that I would be lost without their assistance.

Mealtimes can be quite shaming, but they are nothing to the abject humiliation of their aftermath. Having no recourse but to rely on my manservant to lead me to a chamber pot or privy is mortifying in the extreme. I would wish that indignity on no adult who retains sense enough to recognize the unnaturalness of the situation. I cringe to think of the times when my elimination must have missed its mark. The one mercy of my blindness is that I cannot see the disgust or pity of those who must scour away my mistakes.

As we go on here at Ferndean, we learn daily, and methods for avoiding mishaps are developing. One day while I brooded on a bench under a large oak with Pilot at my feet, John carefully rearranged the rooms I inhabit most frequently so that I would be able to traverse the household without colliding into furnishings. He then took me to every area in turn and explained in detail where each obstacle lay. Although I am getting better at honing a mental map, he continually quizzes me on where I will find various chairs, tables, etc. and how many steps it will take to move among them. If I snap at him impatiently for his insistent prodding of my memory, I hope he understands that my churlishness stems from frustration rather than ingratitude.

Mary, for her part, sewed large buttons onto an old shirt and had John present it to me as a means to practice fastening and unfastening clothing one-handed. He reported her determination that once I master this exercise she will replace the buttons with smaller ones until I am confident enough to dress and disrobe myself. Already I am gaining some skill and am encouraged that I will be capable of more self-reliance before Christmas arrives. It is certain that my father and my brother would be ashamed to see how the walls of convention and reserve between me and my staff have eroded. With no family to help me, I must rely on John and Mary. I pay them well, but knowing that their efforts to encourage and ease me my transition derive from a genuine concern for my welfare somewhat lessens my discomfort with our disrupted social status.

♦

I will never be the man I once was. That is not to say, however, that I cannot become a better man than the Edward Rochester of old. All my life, I viewed religion as having little more value than a social ceremony to keep one in good standing with Society. My dealings with my earthly father hardly disposed me to expect much from my heavenly one. That is not to say I had no sense of right and wrong; instead, I derived much of my moral code from the reading I did at school. The Greeks and the Romans provided me a model for honor, yet did not threaten me with certain doom if I fell short of their ideals. Cicero, Marcus Aurelius, Ovid, and others taught me much about living honorably despite the shortcomings of men around me. Their dictums were my guide, and it was easy to choose the ones that suited me best.

One rainy Sunday afternoon I chanced to be thirsty and decided to test my ability to navigate from my parlor to the kitchen without disturbing John and Mary. Shod in soft slippers, I noiselessly crept down the passageway, thinking to surprise the husband and wife with my accomplishment. Because of the relentless downpour and the difficulties of reaching the small Methodist chapel to which they normally walked, John and Mary had stayed home this Sabbath and honored the day by reading scriptures aloud. When I approached the kitchen, I overheard John intone,

> "And I will bring the blind by a way that they knew not; I will lead them in paths that they have not known: I will make darkness light before them, and crooked things straight. These things will I do unto them, and not forsake them. They shall be turned back; they shall be greatly ashamed, that trust in graven images, that say to the molten images, Ye are our gods. Hear, ye deaf; and look, ye blind, that ye may see."

After the last verse he paused and sighed heavily. In a voice thick with emotion, the man who has known me since childhood proclaimed, "Mary, these words hurt me. I cannot but think of Mr. Edward. He has never been a bad sort despite having little affection or guidance from old Mr. Rochester and Mr. Rowland. True, he has done some wrong things—trying to wed Miss Eyre when he had a wife still living being the worst of them that we know of—yet I cannot wish him ill. I would rest easier if I knew the master accepted that the harsh punishment meted out to him was only to save him from a greater harm, the loss of his eternal soul."

Mary quietly rose from her chair, and I recognized the clatter as she went to the stove and poured two cups of tea. Once settled at the table again, she replied, "John, what you say is right, but you know that Edward Rochester always has been proud of his own learning and is as likely to listen to our counsel as Pilot. We must pray for the master. We must raise up his needs at chapel. We must not, though, lecture him."

Woe to the eavesdropper! I trembled but did not speak as conflicting feelings warred within my breast. Forgetting the thirst that had brought me to the kitchen threshold, I slunk silently back to the parlor and spent the remainder of the afternoon in serious contemplation. Again and again, I reviewed the conversation I had overheard. What had John and Mary said that was not true? I had been arrogant. I had thought myself above the rules of the common man and set my own desires before the principles my innermost self knew to be right. Had not Jane tried to warn me? Had not she argued fervently that man could not create his own set of laws without respect to a greater power? Had not Carter made every effort to dissuade me from attempting a bigamous liaison? As Marcus Aurelius wrote centuries ago, "*Quam facile, amoliri et abstergere visum quodvis vel molestiam excitans vel societati repugnans, et statim in summa tranquillitate esse.*" Determined to have my way, I had gone headlong toward the altar. Doing so had cost me my love, my home, my hand, my sight, and the respect of my peers. Tears trickled from my eye, and my shoulders heaved as I recognized my own willful rush toward destruction, the havoc I had caused for everyone under my responsibility. Did I not deserve every moment of travail I encountered since Thornfield burned? At last my hardened heart was touched and I repented. Being little accustomed to prayer, I could only murmur," Dear God, I have done wrong. I have sinned against you. Please forgive me. Please forgive me." I stayed there in my chair repeating this simple plea till I was exhausted and slept.

VI

This morning Pilot has joined me in the parlor. He sits at my feet enjoying the remains of my breakfast while I stroke his massive head and consider how to pass the day. I wish for something more than my own thoughts to occupy me. It is a pity there is no way for me to read now. John and Mary know their letters and can cipher enough to do the household accounts; however, neither of them is comfortable reading to me from the few books left here through the years. Good fortune intervenes when I hear the door unlatch, and then John says, "Sir, Mr. Carter has come to call. Will you see him?" I agree at once to receive Carter and am gladdened at the prospect of cordial and well-informed company. Admittedly, I have not always welcomed my friend enthusiastically since taking up residence at Ferndean Manor. Indeed, on occasions when my mood was at its darkest John has defied my wishes and brought Carter to me unannounced, knowing that I needed the company and conversation in spite of myself.

Today Carter enters the room with his characteristic brisk stride and greets me heartily while clasping my hand. Pilot yips in happy recognition before obeying John's command to come outside. My medical provider and friend asks how I feel and is pleased to hear that I am doing tolerably well since the stump of my left arm has stopped aching and I am sleeping better. I inquire if Carter has breakfasted and if he is in need of refreshment after his ride. He chuckles and responds that Mrs. Forrester has fed him well this morning and he is quite content.

"Ah, when should I wish you joy, my friend? I begin to suspect your trips to Ferndean Manor have more to do with its relative proximity to the White Hart Inn and Mrs. Forrester than to any concern for my well-being. It is lucky for you that the worthy widow enjoys managing the establishment she inherited from her departed husband and did not decamp for Bath and a life of dissipation upon his demise. Perhaps someday you should hire a conveyance and bring her with you when you call at Ferndean."

Carter laughs merrily and warns me to be careful about my wishes and invitations. When I least expect it, he may spring just such a visit upon me and force me to be charming and gregarious. In a more serious tone, he speaks of Mrs. Forrester and his growing interest and affection for her. He admires her active ways and cheerful manner— as well as her cooking. She has a small son, but that is no obstacle to my friend. He hopes that in time he will find a way to court Mrs. Forrester in earnest. If the young man who has joined Carter in practice lives up to his promise to become a skilled and useful surgeon, Carter finally may be at leisure to pursue personal, rather than merely professional, desires. Having lived frugally throughout his bachelorhood, Carter is comfortably situated and may choose a wife where he likes. I wish him well, even if my innermost self envies his possible marriage, something that is forever denied to me with Jane gone.

Desirous of seeing the changes John mentioned to him before announcing his arrival to me, Carter demands that I give him a tour of the newly improved Ferndean

Manor. I impress him by walking about freely and explaining where each bit of furniture that might impede me stands. He approves of John's efforts and mine. I tell him he has not seen the full extent of my rehabilitation and take him to my room to show him the training shirt Mary has devised for me. Carter claps his hands delightedly and suggests that I grant my servants a bonus for their ingenuity, exclaiming that it does his heart good to find me adapting to my condition. His approval and encouragement are welcome. I sense nothing of pity or false consolation in his words.

The day is sunny and fine, and Carter asks if I would like to walk out of doors for a while. I accept his invitation and allow my hand to rest on his arm when we cross the threshold into the yard. We walk about the property and Carter describes to me what plants are flourishing, which flowers are bursting with color and which fruit trees are budding with a bounty for future enjoyment. We speak generally of our shared interest in botany and then fall into companionable quietude with only the cracking of twigs under our boots and the far-off song of a wren to entertain us.

Clearing his throat, Carter questions me concerning what I can perceive. I tell him my condition is as yet unchanged; I vaguely can detect bright light but little else. He explains that he has written to an ocular specialist explicitly detailing my injuries and seeking an opinion on whether I might someday see more clearly. I hesitantly request that Carter share what the Mayfair specialist has said. Although I want to believe that my sight will be restored, hope can be terrifying in its own way. My friend informs me that the chances are better than we believed at first. It is by no means certain that I shall make out my surroundings plainly again, but it is not impossible. In time, the inflammation which the specialist suspects to cause my blindness may subside to a degree which would allow me some relief. Carter tells me I am to report to him any noticeable improvements or reverses.

Thereafter, we return to the house and Carter, refusing to stand on ceremony, goes to the kitchen to ask Mary for a cool raspberry shrub. Sipping our drinks, we talk of everything and nothing in particular as we rest on the bench situated under the oldest and sturdiest oak at Ferndean. Carter's visit lasts until the sun begins to drop in the sky. With words of encouragement for me and compliments to John and Mary, he mounts his hired hack and turns toward the White Hart Inn. Pilot barks his own goodbyes and must be held to prevent his running after Carter with whom he had passed an agreeable half-hour in fetching a stick while I enjoyed the sounds of their amusement.

VII

I have not experienced a lightning bolt and thunderclap conversion, but I recognize now the part I played in my own disaster. My own stubbornness left my heavenly Father no choice but to smite me mightily in order to save me from wronging and sullying my best beloved. I am ashamed to consider how close I came to putting Jane's soul, as well as my own, in eternal peril. Despite all my best intentions and self-justification, I would have made her a sinner even if we had kept only to one another until parted by death. It is well that she was strong enough to leave me. I cannot bear the thought that I would have made a trollop of her, she who is worth fifty of Celine, Giacinta, and Clara.

Although I accept that I had to be parted from Jane for our future well-being, her absence torments me daily. I am lonely, ever so lonely without her. Gone are the days when I was angry with her for not trusting me and fleeing without a word, or even a hastily scribbled note. Gone are the days when I blamed Mason, Briggs, and Bertha for stopping the wedding. Now I want only one thing. I want my clever, original, and adored little governess to come back to me. If we cannot be married, at least I could then benefit from her friendship and example and show her what it is to be appreciated by a like mind.

VIII

Today my thoughts weigh heavily upon me. I have had another visit from Mr. Quentin, the agent charged with locating Jane. Quentin's efforts have failed again. His network has watched all the port cities carefully, and it is clear that she has not sailed abroad. Descriptions and offers of a reward have been posted in coaching inns throughout Britain, yet no one has come forward. Quentin visited Mrs.

Nasmyth, the former Miss Temple, who had been Jane's cherished mentor at the Lowood Institution, but learned only that their connection had lapsed when the former superintendent left the school. He also conducted a personal interview with Georgiana Reed in London and then sent a counterpart to speak with the Eliza Reed at the nunnery in France. Unfortunately, Quentin came away convinced that Jane's relations know nothing of their unwanted cousin, nor care to know.. Not a single reliable lead has been gleaned from the weekly advertisements placed in newspapers throughout England, Scotland, Ireland and Wales. Occasional replies have led only to liars and pretenders interested in a possible reward. The real Jane Eyre cannot be found, Quentin has declared. He begs me to consider giving up my search, for a year has passed with no success, and he does not like to continue spending my money. I tell him that the search will end when my last farthing is spent. Resigned to my obstinacy, Quentin agrees to search for the elusive Miss Eyre for another half-year although he cannot imagine that doing so will bear results that will give me peace.

Alone after dinner, I sit by the fire and recognize the truth in Quentin's words. Strenuous efforts have been made, yet Jane has not been found. With no family or friends to aid and hide her, I must conclude that my darling girl, through illness or accident, has passed beyond the gates of mortal life. Through each day I suffer great despair and guilt owing to her loss. Tonight I am oppressed with the sensation of how wrong it feels to continue breathing when she does not, when my own selfish plan frightened and drove her to leave behind the place where she was valued and loved. God has been merciful in correcting my immoral ways, but, though grateful, I cannot be happy. Happiness cannot exist for me without Jane.

IX

The hour is late; it must be nigh on midnight. I sit alone in my bedchamber near the open window, feeling a cooling breeze on my cheek and the brush of the light drapery fluttering against me. I strain to see more than an indistinct glow from the moon but without success. From below I hear the rattle of Pilot's collar as he roves about the yard, no doubt searching for invaders to his territory and eager to engage them. My poor canine friend has little entertainment now that I am unable to move about much outdoors without assistance. He must miss the days when he ran alongside Mesrour and me in our travels together, when he sailed abroad and kept me company in many countries.

I am tired and disheartened tonight, but I cannot rest. The world has little to offer me in this present state.

Dependent upon others and unable to contribute as an active member of society, the best I can hope for is that soon I may rejoin Jane in Paradise. Folding my hands in my lap and bowing my head, I pray.

"Oh, heavenly Father, I thank you for granting me salvation. I humbly accept your benevolent wisdom in saving my soul by chastising my flesh. I entreat you now to expand your mercy. If I am not on Earth to meet again with Jane, the one woman who has seen me as I am and loved me regardless, the only woman with whom I could live contentedly, then I beseech you to release me from my humanly existence. Please, Lord, let me come home to you and see dear Jane again. Please do not keep me here in despair much longer. I have been harshly disciplined, and I am truly penitent. I beg you to grant me peace everlasting with Jane at my side in your heavenly kingdom."

My prayer finished, I rest my head on the back of the chair and grip its arms tightly with my five fingers. My heart beats fast in my anguish. One thought only fills my mind. Without conscious choice, I cry out," Jane! Jane! Jane!" A moment later I am stunned and thrilled. From somewhere in the still night I clearly hear my Jane's voice. Her answer to me is this: "I am coming: wait for me . . . Where are you?" Oh God, what is this madness? The accent belongs to none but Jane Eyre. What does it mean? How can it be? Does her spirit truly cry out to mine and whence? Does she tarry in this world or reach for me from another sphere?

X

Four nights ago I sat in this room suffering and cried out my only desire. Nothing more did I ask than to be reunited with Jane in heaven. Tonight I lie in my bed and cannot sleep for joy and disbelief. My heart overflows with gratitude for my merciful Maker, and my mind struggles to comprehend how such a thing came to be. She is here, in this house, under the same roof! It is not a dream or a delusion. My Jane, my precious girl, the best gift I have ever been granted has come back to me!

When she first spoke to me in the parlor this evening, I believed that my mind finally had broken its ties with reality and created a paradise in which Jane continued to exist. Every nerve thrilled with the sensation of some supernatural occurrence and, more than at any moment of the past months, I regretted the loss of my sight. I wanted to see her. I needed to see her. I could not; therefore, I commanded whatever unearthly being that had joined me to speak again. Once more, my ears perceived the voice of Jane Eyre. I thought to myself that surely my madness could not extend to the tangible world, so I frantically reached out for someone of substance. In an instant two small, warm hands wrapped themselves around my right hand. My pulse throbbed in ecstasy. Had I not felt those slender fingers, that smooth palm, that indefinable connection before? Jane! It was Jane! Before she could flit away, I found myself grasping her arm and pulling her to me. Without lascivious intention I groped her shoulder, her neck, her small waist. There could be no mistake. This was my Jane and no other. By instinct I pressed my lips to hers and was rewarded with the well-remembered sensation of her firm lips.

After the first shock had been overcome, Jane explained to me the incredible change in her circumstances. Five thousand pounds! If ever man or woman deserved a full measure of good fortune, it is she. Oh, God, I shall be ever thankful that you have kept her safe this past year! For months I cursed her uncle John Eyre for sending Briggs and Mason to separate us, and now I bless him for making her independent. Surely she would not have come to me as anything other than an equal.

If any doubts lingered regarding the delicious truth that she yet lived in the flesh rather than my imagination, they were dispelled when my dear girl sat with me and shared a simple supper. Afterwards, I quizzed her for some time about her companions and her whereabouts of late. In true Janian fashion, her answers were evasive and she turned our conversation to my uninviting appearance and how she intended to mend it. I wanted to keep her by me until all her wanderings had been revealed. However, she had made an arduous and rapid journey to find me at Ferndean Manor and, assured after months of worry that I was safe and reasonably well, her little body insisted upon a deep sleep. Only a cruel man would have kept her with him talking after she expressed her exhaustion, and I shall never again be cruel to Jane by putting my desires above hers. It was difficult, but I managed to let her leave me on condition that she would resume her tale on the morrow.

I do not know what she meant by laughing so and fleeing when I asked if she had resided with women only since she left Thornfield. The unanswered question pains me as I twist my coverlet and toss from side to side. Could Providence be vindictive enough to bring her back with news that another man intends to have her? I may deserve that torment, but I cannot believe that Jane would punish me thus. Besides, did she not kiss me with a fervor and willingness equal to that of last summer?

I hear Pilot's nails tap across the bare flooring—rugs can trip me, so there are few of them now—outside my door. He pushes the unlatched door ajar and then makes his way to the bedside. "Yes, old fellow, our favourite girl has come home. Is it not miraculous? Are you as pleased as I?" I cannot see him, but I feel the mattress shift under his weight as my steadfast Newfoundland climbs halfway onto the bed in order that I might scratch his solid chest and stroke his ears. He sighs contentedly and licks my hand, something he has not done since my injury. He must sense the change in my frame of mind. He must understand and want to share in my confused bliss. Eventually, Pilot backs away from the bedstead, passes from my bedchamber, and leaves me to my thoughts. I listen carefully and hear creaking as he climbs the stairs and then settles himself in the second floor passage. I smile knowing that he has done his master the favour of locating Jane's room and keeping watch over her until sunrise. There will be no hasty retreats with Pilot stretched across the threshold—even if she did wish to go, which I do not think she does.

Alone in the darkness once more, I ponder how I feel about having my beloved within reach again. I feel extreme elation. I feel wonder that she has forgiven me. I feel renewed hope for my life. I feel with unshakeable conviction that my love for her is unabated. I feel that nothing could be more right than to live out my remaining days with her in an honorable and sanctified marriage—unlike my previous blasphemous attempt. What I do not feel is certainty that she has the same sentiments I harbour in my breast. What brought her here to Ferndean with no word of warning? My darling Jane seems to bear me no grudge for my ill-conceived plot to deceive her last year, but dare I hope that she will have me as her husband? Will she truly tie herself forever to a man who is not vigorous and strong as he was before, or does she pity me and mean to visit only long enough to satisfy herself that I have been redeemed? What of the mysterious household where she has lived since we last were in company? What connections and affections has she forged there? I am plagued by a multitude of perplexing questions that only Jane Eyre can answer.

EPILOGUE

Jane and I have been married ten years this month, and our love is stronger than ever. She and our four children more than compensate me for the physical challenges I face due to the injuries I sustained when Thornfield burned. My life now is better and more blissful than I ever imagined it could be, even in the fevered fantasy world I once planned for us. Rather than settling on the Continent amid strangers to protect my deception, I finally have made a home here in England where I belong. My days are filled with family and friends. I am blessed, and I am content to watch my family grow. I even have regained enough sight to read a few pages at a time. Truly, God is just and loving.

Much has changed since the first year of my marriage to Jane. After the birth of our son, Edward Eyre Rochester, John and Mary, growing old and longing to reunite with their relations for what time they had left on Earth, retired to Derbyshire. They said they had lived to see the Rochesters reinvigorated and thriving at Ferndean Manor, and that was the perfect end to their service. I was sorry to see them go, but granted them an annuity in thanks for their considerable patience and hard work throughout our long association. In their place we welcomed a local couple who have proven their worth time and again.

Not long before the birth of our first daughter, Mary Helen, my old friend Carter wed Catherine Forrester and adopted her son Thomas. The new Mrs. Carter was persuaded to entrust the routine management of the White Hart Inn to someone else; however, to this day she retains the right to veto any practices with which she disagrees. She intends to present the prosperous business to Thomas upon his majority, as his natural father would have wished. Meanwhile, Carter relishes his surgical practice and continues to do much good for those who require his services. We meet often and our children have become great friends.

In the fourth year of our union, Jane and I determined to remove from Ferndean Manor. We had been happy there but decided that it was unwise to risk our children's health in the unwholesome damp that clings to the spot nearly year round. We surprised many when we announced our intentions to rebuild on the site of Thornfield Hall's ruins. Returning to the orchards and fields I have loved since boyhood and making a new start there was the right choice for us, nonetheless. The unhappy times and sorrow of the old house are all but forgotten. Our present residence is a modern, convenient building large enough to accommodate comfortably all the visitors we receive throughout the year. It may be less stately than the edifice that once stood here, but it is by far the better home.

Furthermore, I have taken great pleasure in reconnecting with my tenants and bringing the farming practices on the property up to date. I fancy the labourers like the increased productivity and prefer having an interested landowner to one who is distant and sends an agent to do his business. I confess there was some agitated talk amongst the locals when I reappeared in Hay to arrange for the building of the new house. However, in due course my past wickedness was forgiven when my neighbors—with the exception of the sullen Dowager

Ingram and her fading eldest daughter, of course—observed the upright, quiet life and earnest church attendance that have become my normal existence with a loving partner at my side. One pensioner of my estate, made bold by age and a glass of beer, remarked on Lady Day the year after I resumed my place that he was "cheered to see the Fairfax blood show at last." Where Arthur Rochester would have had the man removed from his cottage for such an affront, Edward Fairfax Rochester, at peace with himself, grinned and accepted the compliment.

Our second daughter, Diana Maria, and our second son, John Rivers Rochester, unfortunately came to us too late to know faithful old Pilot, who had been delighted to rove again in the open fields he once knew. My loving Newfoundland dog finally closed his eyes one autumn afternoon and did not wake, much to the grief of the entire household. He reposes now under the regenerating horse-chestnut tree in the orchard, the very same tree struck by lightning long ago. A simple marker denotes his grave. Pilot's place in our affections has not been taken and cannot be by any other pet, but every effort to do so is being made by Bounce and Sassy, a raucous pair of spaniels who delight and vex us in turn with their lively antics.

Having no remaining close family of my own, I have embraced Jane's cousins and their husbands. I anticipate with great pleasure our rotating visits, for wives and husbands alike are intelligent, thoughtful and decent people. Our conversations are varied and instructive. Never do they stoop to gossip. I wish I had known them all earlier in my life. The Fitzjameses and the Whartons are truly good, and I enjoy their company almost as much as I do my quiet time with darling Jane, who remains my most cherished love and my *raison d'être.*

Adele, despite my cynical fears in her early days, has grown into a lovely young woman. She has finished her regular education and now studies with a renowned teacher of music in London. She, too, will go to the stage someday but as an acclaimed and gifted soprano. Not only is her voice powerful and sweet, but her knowledge of French and ability to pick up other languages easily is an advantage. Unlike her mother, Adele is carefully chaperoned and has an allowance which she tends carefully. I shall never be certain of her paternity, but—after serious discussion with my astute and compassionate wife—I have set aside a bequest for Adele so that she never will be forced to choose between her virtue and an empty stomach if her career does not proceed as she hopes.

Adele visits my family as often as her *maestro* allows, and we are glad to have her among us. All the children clamor for her attention and view her as a sort of glamorous older cousin. Both sons declare they shall marry her when they are old enough; both daughters delight in having Adele brush and style their hair in the newest modes from the capitol. She, meanwhile, loves to regale Edward, John, Mary, and Diana with stories of the days when their mamma taught a pampered, flighty French girl history and arithmetic. Adele continues to cherish an abiding affection for her former governess, and they are quite merry together when they tease me about my moody ways of old. No more do the pair regard the master of the house with awe. Instead, they mockingly insist that I provide the evening's entertainment in payment for the nights of impatient gloom to which I subjected them more than a decade ago. After dinner is eaten and the children are abed, I often am compelled to sing as one of them accompanies me at the piano. It is a pleasurable punishment.

Yes, all is well with me as I creep toward old age. I have

few bodily complaints and mental worries, and none of them are serious. Even so, more often as the years pass, there are nights when I awaken from dreams vivid and haunting—visions of a time when I was a different man and had different hopes, memories of a place exotic and strange to me. In those breathless moments upon first waking, I am lost in place and time. Before I can slow my breathing, settle into my pillow again and slumber, I must turn and confirm which woman lies beside me in the dark. In truth, now and again I half-expect to find a young and beautiful Bertha Mason gazing up at me with dark and knowing eyes, for once I was her husband and she was the first Mrs. Rochester.

ABOUT THE AUTHOR

A native of West Tennessee, M. C. Smith is a graduate of Christian Brothers University in Memphis, Tennessee. She lives in Durham, North Carolina where she works for a national not-for-profit agency.

Made in the USA
Charleston, SC
23 December 2013